Wizard for a day

Other Apple Paperbacks
you will enjoy:

Forest
by Janet Taylor Lisle

My Dog Can Fly!
by Leigh Tresseder

Wizard's Hall
by Jane Yolen

The Day the Fifth Grade Disappeared
by Terri Fields

Wizard for a day

Original Title: *Denzil's Dilemma*

Sherryl Jordan

AN
APPLE
PAPERBACK

SCHOLASTIC INC.
New York Toronto London Auckland Sydney

ISBN 0-590-22283-X

12 11 10 9 8 7 6 5 4 3 2 1   6 7 8 9/9 0 1/0

Printed in the U.S.A.   40

First Scholastic printing, December 1996

*For Ann and Paddy
who celebrate the magic
and the beauty
in the world*

Contents

Wizard for a day

One day Sherryl Jordan was talking to her frend, Jean Bennett. [Sherryl is the one who holds the pen— Im the wizzard who makes the reel magic]. They wer talking about me and Jean sed: "Woodnt it bee fun if Denzil took Sam back to <u>his</u> wirld."

I got reely exited about that idea — Id thawt about it myself a few times. Luckilee Sherryl got exited about it too and between us we got Sam back to my place. We had a marveliss time even thow things did get a little bit out of control.

Im writting this to thank Jean for her wunderfol idea.

Thank yoo Jean.

With greetings from

Denzil

1 The First Problem

he stones of the old bridge were treacherous with ice. The donkey stopped, refusing to cross. Denzil tugged gently at the rope about the animal's neck, and spoke soft words of encouragement.

"There'll be a warm blanket for you when we get home," Denzil said. "And two carrots and some hay."

The donkey lowered its eyes, stiffened its legs, and refused to be bribed. "I'll whack your rump if you don't cross," said Denzil, less softly.

The donkey snorted, its breath making puffs of steam in the freezing air. Snow began to fall in shining flakes on Denzil's unruly black hair and on the dark firewood tied across the donkey's back.

"If you don't move," said Denzil, pulling harder on the rope, "I'll leave you here in the snow, and go home by myself."

The donkey looked at him from under its long lashes, and sneered. Denzil shivered, blowing on his cupped hands to warm them. He wore mittens, but they had holes in them. His right hand, with the donkey's rope wound firmly about it, was numb with cold. Even though he wore a thick woollen cloak and handmade leather boots, he was chilled to the bone. He longed for home, for hot soup and a roaring fire. But he couldn't go back without the firewood and the donkey. And the donkey knew that.

"I'll find a way to move you," muttered Denzil. He looked at the road behind them, down towards the distant trees. Through the snow they looked grey and ghostly. The road, the Great Wood, and the white fields all around, were deathly quiet.

Denzil's green eyes glittered, became narrow and intense. He frowned slightly, his whole being concentrated on a single thought, the seed of a sound; a pattern of power that arched across the wintry ground between himself and the trees. In his mind he spoke the magic words:

"Out of the silence,
Out of the white,
Sounds of defiance,
Howls of the night —
Sounds to chasten!
Sounds to chill!
Hounds to hasten
A beast too still!"

For a moment nothing happened. Then, slowly, the snowflakes near the forest seemed to gather together, to form into strange, thin patterns that flew through

2

the air towards the boy and his donkey. Unearthly sounds came with the swirling snow; long, fearsome howls of hunger and defiance and rage. They were the howls of wild wolves.

The donkey's ears pricked; its eyes rolled back, white and terrified; and it took off across the bridge as if all the fiends in the world were after it.

Immediately, Denzil knew this hadn't been a good idea. He suspected it the moment he began to be dragged behind the panic-stricken beast, his hand still twisted about the donkey's rope; he was fairly sure of it when he fell and started skidding flat on his stomach across the icy bridge; he was even more certain when the sticks of firewood worked loose and started falling off, hitting him one at a time over the head as they bounced past; and he knew it with devastating conviction when he finally got his hand loose from the rope, letting it go just as they dashed madly around a corner by the mill-pond. The donkey went one way and Denzil went the other — straight into the icy pond. He did an admirable slide on his belly across the frozen rim, then the ice shattered under his weight, and he plunged in.

I really don't like winter much, thought Denzil, as he turned himself into a water-rat, scrambled easily back onto the thin ice and scuttled to the shore. He sat on the edge of the road by a stick of firewood, and concentrated on being himself again. Slowly his ratty face turned pink and lost all its whiskers and fur. His neck grew thin and long, while his shoulders became the strong, bony shoulders of a boy of twelve. Shivering violently, he hitched up his ragged hose, drew his wet cloak closer about him, and stood gloomily watching his donkey disappear into the distance, firewood scattering the white road behind it.

Strictly speaking, it wasn't Denzil's donkey at all; it was Valvasor's. Valvasor was very fussy about his donkey and didn't like it being driven too hard. It'd arrive home now panting and sweating from fright and exhaustion, with no firewood and no one looking after it — and Denzil, as usual, would take all the blame.

"I don't think I like animals much, either," said Denzil, beginning the long tramp home, and picking up as much firewood as he could on the way.

As he neared the cottages of his village, he saw the boys and girls out in the snow. They were building a snowman and had almost finished it. Grand it was, with a carrot for a nose, stones for eyes, a hat, and two broomsticks for arms. Someone had put mistletoe on the hat, because there were only six days to Christmas.

Denzil stood to watch, his arms aching with cold and the weight of the firewood he'd saved, and he longed to go and help them.

One of the boys building the snowman noticed Denzil, and stopped. He nudged the boy next to him and they both stared at Denzil. Soon all the children

4

were staring and silent, watching the boy with the strange green eyes and wild black hair, who was apprentice to the great wizard Valvasor. The children had heard talk of Denzil; heard talk of his magic power, which, some mothers whispered, was almost as great as the power of Valvasor himself.

"We've heard things about you!" called one of the boys, and his friends hissed at him to be quiet. But the boy, seeing that Denzil didn't move, went on. "They say that you turned into a bird and flew to another world. And they say you tamed a monster called Kar, and rode him through a city a thousand times bigger than our village, and fought a mighty black dragon called Trayne."

The children, like coloured statues against the snow, stood as still as their snowman. Their eyes were fixed on Denzil's face.

"Leave him, Rowl," whispered a boy. "Don't vex him. He'll turn you into a toad or something."

Rowl grinned, and stuck his thumbs into his fine leather belt. He was bigger than the others, and wore a cloak trimmed with grey fur. Denzil knew him; he was the mole-catcher's son, and was well known for his arrogance and daring. He went poaching for pheasants in the village lord's forest, and risked a whipping for it. But he was never caught.

"Wizards' apprentices don't scare me," Rowl said. "Come on, Denzil. Tell us about that mighty dragon you killed. Show us your muscles. If you've got any."

One of the other boys shook Rowl's sleeve, and tried to drag him away. Afraid, the younger children crept off and disappeared into their cottages and shut the doors. Denzil saw their faces staring out between the wooden window shutters before their mothers pulled them inside again. He turned to go on to his own home, but Rowl called him back.

"We heard about the knights you saw, too," said Rowl. "The knights who fought with swords of light, and who rode silver horses through the skies. Are you as good at magic as you are at telling lies?"

Denzil tried hard not to listen. He started walking away again, but something hard and cold hit him in the middle of the back, almost making him drop the bundle of firewood. He turned around. Rowl was making another snowball. When it was hard enough, he aimed it at Denzil's face. It missed his face, but hit him firmly in the chest, knocking him back a step. Rowl smiled, though there was only challenge in his eyes, and bitterness. Only two friends were with Rowl now, and they were nervous.

"I don't lie," said Denzil quietly. "And who told you of Trayne?"

"I heard it from Mother Wyse," said Rowl, grinning. "Old Battybird. I was hiding outside her house, and heard her telling Valvasor."

Denzil gulped. "Valvasor? She told *him*? When?"

Rowl's grin widened, not pleasantly, and he would not say.

6

Denzil's face went white, and he felt weak and sick. He started walking again, stumbling, hardly seeing where he went.

"Hey! Wizard!" Rowl yelled after him. "Friends with the old witch, are you? Do you swap spells with her too, or only stories?"

Denzil didn't even hear.

His head spun with the awful news he had heard — that Valvasor knew about the journey Denzil had made; that he must know, too, about the sacred charm he'd stolen, and the forbidden, powerful magic that had flung Denzil to another world seven hundred years into the future.

Only one person had Denzil told about Sam MacAllister and her strange, modern world with its cars and motorbikes, computers and videos, and the terrible black dragon called a train. He'd told Mother Wyse.

"I trusted her," muttered Denzil to himself, almost weeping with despair and anguish. "I *trusted* her! And she told the one person I didn't ever want to find out. It's a wonder he hasn't killed me by now. Or turned me into a chicken and cooked me. Or . . . oh, gawd, maybe my punishment's still to come. What if he's waiting for me now with some dreadful spell half worked . . ."

He couldn't bear to think about it. He had an almost overwhelming desire to run away, to never have to face Valvasor again, but he knew that was useless.

Valvasor could turn himself into a mist, and go everywhere and see everything. There was no escaping him. And no deceiving him either, it seemed, especially with friends like Mother Wyse betraying all your secrets.

That hurt Denzil more than anything — her betrayal. Denzil had few enough friends as it was, because all the village children were afraid of him. The only one who wasn't afraid of him was Rowl, and he hated Denzil.

Apprehensive, not knowing whether to face the wizard or to flee, Denzil came to Valvasor's house. The donkey was in its little stable outside, but the door was still open and the animal was not brushed or tended to. It was quivering with cold. Denzil too was quivering, but with more than cold. He stopped outside the massive door of his home, chewing his lower lip, feeling his heart banging like a drum inside his ribs. Slowly, he pushed open the door and crept inside.

The fire had gone out, and the one big room of the house was gloomy with shadows. Denzil glanced at the carved bed in one corner; it was empty. He looked at the great wooden table where Valvasor mixed his potions, carved amulets, and occasionally wrote magic spells in books for Denzil to have later on. The table too was bare, its candles gone out. He looked at the huge carved chair near the fireplace, and at the loft high up under the roof where Valvasor sometimes went to work his deepest, most sacred and secret business. It was deserted. Valvasor was out.

Denzil heaved a sigh of relief, crossed the wooden floor, and threw the firewood down on the wide stone hearth. He lit the fire using the dry wood already there, and when the flames leapt he stripped off all his wet clothes, spread them out near the fire to dry, and put on clean ones from the wooden chest against one wall. He pulled on dry boots, and went outside to give the donkey its carrots and a warm blanket, and to shut the stable door against the snow and wind.

Then he went inside again and sat in the wizard's carved chair to plot a way out of his trouble.

* * *

Sam MacAllister stared at herself in the mirror, frowning.

"The wings aren't right," she said, turning around and looking back over her shoulder. "They're too big. Everyone else has got little ones."

"They're not too big," said her mother, putting a few more pins in the hem of Sam's white gown. "They're beautiful wings. It took me a week to make all those silk feathers and sew them onto the wire frames. And the sequins give them a kind of shine, like the shine of peacock's wings."

"I'm supposed to be an angel, not a peacock," grumbled Sam.

"Stop fidgeting, or you'll get pins in your ankles," said her mother. "And for goodness' sake, put Murgatroyd down. If he does anything disgusting on your dress, he'll ruin it. He should be in his cage, anyway. I thought we made some rules about not having your rat in the house."

"Only when Grandma's here," said Sam, putting Murgatroyd on the dressing-table, and smiling while he climbed into her mother's open jewellery box. "Besides," went on Sam, "Dad's fumigating my treehouse for fleas, so Murgatroyd can't stay in there at the moment. He'd get sick."

"He'll get sick if he eats my pearl earrings," said Mrs MacAllister with her lips almost closed across a line of pins. "Do something with him, Sam. And stand still just for a minute. I've nearly finished."

Sam dragged Murgatroyd away from the rings and pearls, and put him carefully on her head, like a crown. Then she lowered her arms and stood very still while her mother finished her hem.

"That'll do," said Mrs MacAllister, standing up and inspecting the hem. "I'll sew it up tonight, while I'm watching television. You really do look wonderful, Sam. With your golden hair and blue eyes, you look just like a real angel — except for the peanut butter all over your face, and that rat on your head. Wash your face, then come out to the garden and we'll take a photo."

Sam sighed but knew better than to argue.

Mrs MacAllister went to the kitchen to hunt for the camera, and Sam went to the bathroom and wiped peanut butter all over a towel. Then she went outside. Her brother, Travis, was in the driveway working on his old car. He'd had a lot of trouble with it lately, and spent more time fixing it than he did driving it.

"You should have kept your motorbike," said Sam, peering over Travis's shoulder, careful not to get her snow-white robes next to his overalls.

"I couldn't keep it," muttered Travis from the oily darkness under the bonnet. "Felicity hated the motorbike, especially in the rain. That's why I got this thing."

"You should have got a new girlfriend, instead," said Sam. "That would have been easier, and cheaper."

Travis chuckled. "Wise child," he said, and went on with his work.

Sam went to swing on the clothesline. She whirled majestically, flying, her wings shining in the sun. But Murgatroyd dropped dizzily down the front of her dress and she had to stop to rescue him. She looked across the lawn at the tree at the far end of their section. She could just see her treehouse, almost lost in the shadowy pine, and could hear her father scrambling around inside. She heard a few grunts and growls, and suspected the fleas were winning the war.

It was funny, the way adults worried about little things like rats and fleas. That was one of the things Sam had loved about Denzil when he was here; he'd loved all the things she loved — had even turned himself into a rat a few times, and into a flea. Sam smiled to herself, remembering.

He was her own special wizard from long ago, wild and wonderful and marvellously wicked. He'd been accidentally transported to Sam's place, and was unable to go back. She'd found him in her garden — at the very place she was standing now — and had hidden him for a while in her treehouse. But he'd gone back, after a great deal of bother and difficulty, to his own time. Sam missed him terribly.

"Travis," she called, remembering something else, and Travis looked up from the car. His face was smeared with oil. He looked hot in his heavy overalls, and his hair was damp with sweat. "What, Sam?" he asked.

"Didn't Denzil say something about coming back at Christmas?"

"He said it as a joke," said Travis. "Just to make us all worried."

"It wouldn't worry me," said Sam.

"Me neither," said Travis with a grin. He ducked under the bonnet again. Sam stood stroking Murgatroyd. She felt too warm in the long gown. The sun pricked her bare arms and made Murgatroyd pant.

For some odd reason, Sam thought of snow.

2 Sam's Swift Surprise

enzil sat in the carved chair, gnawed his nails, and stared at the fire. The thing that worried him most was Valvasor's silence. If the wizard knew about Denzil's wickedness, why hadn't he said anything?

"He must be so mad he can't talk about it," thought Denzil, distraught. "He must be secretly thinking up the worst punishment that was ever invented. He must think I'm the wickedest person alive. He must think I'm a liar and a thief. And I'm not. I'm a burglar, but not a thief. And I didn't burgle the sacred charm, not really. I just borrowed it. But he won't believe me if I tell him. He'll never believe me again."

Denzil groaned, slumped in the great chair, and covered his face with his hands. Suddenly he shot bolt upright.

"Sam!" he cried, his face aglow, almost laughing in his excitement. "Sam could tell him I only borrowed it! Sam would tell him I'm not really wicked! Sam

13

would stick up for me! She wouldn't let him punish me! Sam —"

He jumped up and ran to the door. Then he stopped, the joy dying on his face. He leaned against the door and sighed. It was no good rushing out to find his one and only friend in all the world. She wasn't even in his world — she was seven centuries away.

Or was she?

Denzil's eyes slid to the books of magic stacked on the shelves behind the table. The firelight glimmered on them, shining on the gold letters on the old leather spines — letters that spelled out mysteries and magic, beginnings and ends, and awesome journeys . . .

Slowly, Denzil went over to the books. He pulled one down, put it on the table, and opened it. He took one of the massive candles over to the fire, lit it, then took it back to the table and set it down beside the book. He looked at the spells headed 'Reuniting Friends'.

He saw something interesting and leaned closer, panting with excitement and fear. "I could do it," he murmured. "It's a short spell. But she'd have to be thinking of me, too, while I was thinking about her. There has to be a connection. I've got to somehow send her the words to say, and she's got to say them at the same time I do. Oh, Sam . . ."

Something banged in the dim room, and Denzil spun around, terrified. But it was only the wind banging a wooden window shutter. He closed the shutter and went back to the book. He took a sheet of parchment and a quill and ink from a drawer in the table, then started copying out the spell.

It was not as difficult as the spell he'd made eight months ago; this one was called a Connecting-Word, and it worked by connecting people's thoughts and minds. This spell didn't have sums and other troublesome calculations; it worked through people's intuitions and imaginings, and had a power altogether different. The spell would be fairly easy for Denzil; the tricky bit would be to get Sam to do her part.

When he'd copied out the Connecting-Word, Denzil rolled the parchment carefully and slid it inside his shirt, next to his thumping heart.

"Outside," he said to himself. "I've got to be outside to do it. I don't think she'd appreciate being flown in through a thatched roof at the speed of a century per second. Besides, she could end up in the cauldron. She wouldn't like being dunked in soup, even if it is chicken and tastes great. I'd better be careful . . ."

He glanced across the floor at the huge, shadowy cupboard that housed all Valvasor's most precious belongings: his dried plants for medicines, his crystals, magic stones, sacred bones, and his most powerful magic charms.

Denzil took a deep breath. He got the key to the cupboard and unlocked the massive carved doors. His hand went straight to the gold and silver medallion hanging from a leather thong on a tiny hook. He took the talisman down, amazed again at the way it blazed with a light all its own and was warm in his hands. Gold on one side and silver on the other, it symbolised the sun and moon and the everlasting circle of time. Inside, it held a lock of Noah's beard.

Denzil lifted the medallion to his lips and kissed it reverently. Then he closed his eyes and out of the marvellous lights and shades of memory, he recalled Sam's face.

"I hope you're nearly ready, Sam," he said.

* * *

"You'll have to wait a minute, Sam, while I get this thing focused," said Mrs MacAllister coming into the garden, the camera in her hands. "And take Murgatroyd off your head. Angels have halos, not rats, hovering about their heads."

"He's not hovering, he's hanging on," said Sam. And she suspected he was doing more than that; there was something warm trickling down behind her ear. She didn't dare move, in case something dripped down onto her pure white gown. That was another thing adults were funny about.

Mrs MacAllister fiddled a bit more with the camera, and Sam looked at her watch. It was a red Mickey Mouse watch, and Sam treasured it because Grandad had given it to her the day before he died.

"Hurry up, Mum," said Sam. "It's nearly two o'clock. Dad said he'd take me and Janey swimming, at two."

"I bet he's forgotten," murmured Mrs MacAllister. She finally got the camera focused, and told Sam to say cheese.

"Can't," said Sam. "I'll get Murgatroyd excited. Can I say something else instead, if it rhymes with you-know-what?"

"Say anything you like," said her mother, "but smile while you say it."

Sam thought for a while. "I need Denzil," she said. "He was very good at making up poems, especially spells."

"You do not need Denzil," said her mother, peering at Sam through the camera lens. "You need a smile on your face, and that rat out of the front of your dress."

Sam fished Murgatroyd out, and stood very still with him cradled in her hands. She smiled, thinking of Denzil all dressed up in a black silk dressing-gown and pink tights, and yelling something about wings of bats and acrobats.

Suddenly, the weirdest words came winging into Sam's mind.

> *In awesome flight*
> *Through time and space,*
> *With second sight*
> *I see your face.*
> *Our memories merge,*
> *Our minds unite,*
> *Our paths converge*
> *In ageless light.*

17

By wondrous rite
And sacred vow,
True friends unite
In timeless NOW!

Sam repeated the words, smiling to herself, thinking how fine they sounded. Suddenly, she began to feel incredibly light. She thought at first that she was fainting, or flying, and was terribly alarmed; then she felt as if she were being lifted high, and it was such a marvellous feeling that she laughed and started singing.

"Sam!" cried her mother. "Stop waving your arms about! Sam! *Sam!*" Her voice rose to a scream.

Alarmed, Travis lifted his head just in time to see his mother fainting on the grass. And he saw Sam, angel-white and shining, lift her arms to the summer light . . . and disappear.

* * *

Denzil stood in the snow behind Valvasor's house, the parchment clutched in his hands, and stared. The snow was brilliant. White light shone all around, so bright it almost blinded him. Glorious it was, unearthly and shimmering, and warm. Then, out of the very heart of the light, her hair golden and her face full of joy, came Sam.

Sam with a white gown and angel's wings.

"Oh, gawd!" howled Denzil, horrified. "I've killed

her! Oh, sweet Jesus, Mother Mary, Saint Theresa! Save me! I've done a wicked murder!"

And he fell on the ground, sobbing.

Bewildered, Sam watched him for a while, wondering where she was. Freezing wind hissed across her bare arms, and her feet ached in the whiteness on the ground. She felt dizzy with the cold, and her eyes could hardly bear the brightness all around. After a few moments she realised that she stood in snow. And there was a great stone house behind Denzil; a house with wooden shutters instead of glass in the windows, and a thatched roof dripping melted snow and icicles.

"You've brought me to your world," she said, amazed, half smiling.

Slowly, Denzil lifted his head. His face was as pale as the paper he held crushed to his chest. His hands shook. Sam inspected him, noticing that he'd grown a bit. He was wearing a rough woven brown tunic, and handmade leather shoes with long pointed toes. He had a grey hat with a peak dangling down the back, and it fitted right around his face like a balaclava, with a wide collar that covered his shoulders. His thin legs were covered with woollen grey hose, patched on the knees with dirty yellow squares.

Sam grinned. "I suppose the pink tights don't fit you anymore," she said.

Denzil gulped. "I'm sorry, Sam," he choked. "Please forgive me."

"Doesn't worry me," she said. "You looked silly in ballet tights, anyway."

"Not the tights. You. I'm sorry about you."

Sam's grin vanished. "What do you mean, sorry?" She was quiet for a while, staring at him, while a fear colder than the snow settled across her heart.

"Are you telling me that this is a mistake?" she asked. "That I'm not supposed to be here, after all? That you've been dabbling in spells too big for you, and now it's my turn to be stuck somewhere hundreds of years away from home?"

Denzil shrank back against the stone wall. "Don't be angry, Sam," he whimpered. "Please. I didn't know. I must have got it wrong again. I . . . " Sam's blue eyes narrowed. Murgatroyd squeaked in her hands, and she put him up onto her left shoulder. He sat there shivering. Sam had been shivering too, a second ago, but now she felt hot with rage.

"If you've messed things up again, Denzil, I'll make you really sorry. Mum's supposed to be taking a photo of me. It takes her half an hour to get that camera sorted out, and just when she finally gets it right, I disappear. That's rotten timing. I thought you'd be a better wizard by now. I thought you'd have your spells sorted out — have your magic a bit more under control. Well, you're just as bad at it as ever."

"And you're just as snappish as ever, Sammy Snarlybritches!" he yelled, standing up, and going over to face her. "I bet you're not even a good angel!

20

I bet they've got a special place for crosspatches like you, somewhere just inside the Pearly Gates, where nobody stays for long! I bet you don't even get to see the saints! I bet they make you polish the harps! I bet — "

"I'm not an angel!" she cried. "I'm me! Sam!"

"Didn't think you were!" he sniffed. "Your wings are falling off. They haven't got real feathers, either. Bet you can't even fly as well as I can."

"I can't fly at all," she said, wriggling her shoulders where the straps were slipping. "I'm not an angel, Denzil. I'm just dressed up as one for our school play. The wings are make-believe. Mum made them for me."

"You're not dead then?"

"I hope not. I thought I was just visiting you. Isn't this your world?"

"Yes."

"Did you try to bring me here?"

"Yes. That's what the spell was for."

"So it worked?"

"Must have. You're here, aren't you?"

"I suppose I am. I'm certainly not at home with Mum taking a photo of me."

A slow smile spread across Denzil's face. "Welcome to Northwood Village," he said.

"Thanks for inviting me," said Sam.

"Sorry I couldn't call you first," said Denzil. "We're a bit slow getting phones here."

Sam wasn't listening. She was staring at the corner of the house, her eyes wide with astonishment.

A woman stood there, with a fat white goose struggling in her arms. She wore a long, rough brown dress and a white apron. She too wore headgear that covered her shoulders, though hers was made of softer material and embroidered on the edges. Her stockings were wrinkled about her ankles, and were knitted in stripes of black and orange wool. Her cheeks were bright red with the cold, and her hands, as they held the straining goose, were shaking.

"Mother Goodhart," stammered Denzil. "Oh, blimey."

Mother Goodhart dropped the goose and slowly sank to the ground.

"Good Lord preserve us," she said, in hushed and prayerful tones. She bowed low, covering her face with her apron. "An angel has visited our village."

Sam started to giggle.

Denzil bit his lower lip, and wondered whether he should make a forgetting-spell for Mother Goodhart.

But before he could remember it, Mother Goodhart slowly stood up, her hands clasped in joy and adoration. She looked one last time on the angel's face, then fled after the escaped goose, to tell all of Northwood about the heavenly visitation.

"Well," said the angel to Denzil, "are you going to give me some clothes to warm me up, or do I have to stand out here and do aerobics?"

3 *Hiding Sam*

enzil bent over the wooden chest and pulled out a grubby pair of hose and a woollen shirt. "Try these," he said.

Sam took the hose between her finger and thumb, holding them at arm's length. "Don't you ever wash your clothes?" she asked.

"What for?" asked Denzil, bending over the chest again and almost falling in. He surfaced at last, puffing after his efforts, with another shirt. This was linen, almost white, with embroidery around the cuffs and hem.

"This was Valvasor's," said Denzil, "when he was young. It's nice, if you like old-fashioned stuff."

Sam stared at him, standing there in his medieval pointed shoes, hand-knitted hose, and ancient woven shirt; and she smiled.

"I'd really like to look as ultramodern as you do," she said. "Haven't you got anything posh for me?"

Denzil stared down at his own clothes, pleased. "I could burgle something for you," he said. "Mistress

Morgin made her girls new dresses last winter. I'll get one of those for you."

Before Sam could stop him, he'd raced out of the house, banging the door after him.

Sam sat down on a fur rug by the fire, and waited. The house was silent and empty with Denzil gone. She felt uneasy and afraid. There were too many shadows in this house, and the firelight leaping over the walls made things in the cupboards and shelves seem alive and moving. Books seemed to glow, and paintings on the plaster walls wavered and changed. She was sure one picture was of the sea and a sailing-ship; the next moment it was the sky and a bird flying. In the darkness high above, the beams seemed alive with fluttering things, and she was sure she could see eyes staring down on her.

Sam shivered, drew up her knees and put her arms about them, and wriggled closer to the fire. The door was flung open and Denzil appeared, spotted with snow, and bearing a bundle of blue. He brought it over and dropped it on the floor at Sam's feet.

"I got the best one," he said.

"Didn't take you long," she said, unfolding the bundle.

"I flew. When I got there I turned myself into a mouse. It's easy being a burglar, when you're a mouse. You can creep in anywhere. They were all out getting their corn ground at the mill, so their cottage was empty. Do you like it?"

Sam was holding up the blue dress against her. It was a bit too big, but everyone wore loose-fitting clothes here. There was a white apron to go with it, and red hose. He'd even stolen some shoes for her, though they had holes in the long pointed toes and smelled a bit.

"Well, put them on," said Denzil. "I'll go and hide your angel things in the stable. They'll be safe there; Valvasor leaves all the donkey work to me."

When Denzil came back, Sam was dressed in her second-hand clothes. "Where are the buttons and zips?" she asked.

Denzil looked blank.

"You know," she said, irritably. "I can't go around with the back undone."

"Ah!" said Denzil, and dived into the chest again. This time he came up with a ball of wool and a bone needle. He gave them to Sam. "Sew yourself in," he said.

"What? How do I get out of it?"

"What do you want to get out of it for? You just got in."

"Well, I'll need to get undressed for baths, and for sleeping."

Denzil grinned. "Not here you don't. No baths here. Only at Christmas. But I had three at your place, so I don't need another one for years. You've had so many you'll be clean until your teeth fall out."

Sam looked disgusted, and thrust the needle and

wool into his hands. "Here. I can't reach the back. You sew it up."

The grin vanished from Denzil's face. "*What?* Me do sewing?"

"Well, if you won't, I'll ask Valvasor," said Sam.

Muttering and squinting like a goblin in the firelight, Denzil threaded the needle and sewed up the back of Sam's dress. When he had finished she pulled on the strange pointed shoes, and twirled around, feeling the heavy woven skirt brush the scratchy stockings on her legs.

Her clothes scratched everywhere; the thick seams, sewn by hand with heavy threads, made uncomfortable ridges across her shoulders and down her back. The seam Denzil had sewn was terribly rough, and the material rubbed on the spots where he'd pricked her with the needle.

"I don't like them," she said.

"Tough," said Denzil. "They're on until summer."

She shot him a sharp, suspicious look. "It's already summer," she said, "in the place you're sending me back to *tomorrow.*" The way she said 'tomorrow' made him feel nervous.

"Valvasor will be home soon," he said. "You'd better hide. I'll come and get you when the time's right."

"When will that be?" she asked.

"When Valvasor's in a good mood," he replied.

"In half an hour or so?"

Denzil gave her an odd little smile, and shrugged.

In half a year, if we're lucky, he thought. Aloud, he said: "Soon. You can go and hide in the stable."

"I'm not going to the stable," she said. "I'll hide in that little room up there under the roof."

"You can't," said Denzil. "Nobody's allowed there. Even Valvasor goes there only to do special spells."

"It'll be a good place to hide then," said Sam.

"But you can't get up there."

"Why not? There's a ladder."

"You won't be able to climb it."

"Why?"

"You're a girl."

Sam snorted, settled Murgatroyd into the deep pocket in her apron, and began to climb up the rickety ladder.

Denzil stood at the bottom, biting his nails. "Don't touch anything up there, Sam," he said. "That's a special place. Valvasor does his highest magic up there. And don't make a noise. I'll get him in a good mood, and then you can tell him why I sto— borrowed his magic charm. He'll believe you. Don't forget to tell him how clever and brave I was, and how helpful I was to your mother and father. He'll be very impressed with that."

"Helpful? *You* helpful?" said Sam, peering down at Denzil over the edge of the floor, and grinning.

He pulled a face, and went to get a thick fur from one of the huge chests near Valvasor's bed. He took it up to Sam. "I think you'll be warm enough," he said.

"If you're not, tomorrow night I'll turn you into a bug or something, and you can sleep on the hearth by me. It's warm there."

"No thanks," she said. "Bugs get squashed."

"I could un-squash you," he said. "I'd turn back Time to the second before you were mashed, and save you."

Sam wasn't impressed with that idea at all. "If you change just one little bit of me," she said, "I'll thump you."

"Won't hurt, if you've got a ladybug's arms," he teased.

Sam went to grab him by the shirt, but he shot over the side of the loft and slid down the ladder, laughing.

At that moment there was a stamping outside, and the door of the house flew open. In a gust of wind and a whirl of snow a man came in, his emerald robes swinging wildly about him. He slammed the door shut and turned around, his eyes bright like fires above his dark beard, his face fierce and noble like a king's.

"I have heard news, apprentice of mine," he said, and his voice was like quiet thunder in that darkening room. "There is talk in our village of a visitor. A strange and shining visitor."

"There is, master?" said Denzil, trying to sound casual. The words came out like a startled squeak.

"There is indeed," said Valvasor.

Sam listened, shrinking into the blackness at the far end of the loft. Something small and hairy ran over her wrist, but she didn't dare move.

"Furthermore," said Valvasor, his voice as soft as snow falling in the deepest night, "there is talk in our village, Denzil, of you."

There was a heavy silence then, and Sam could hear Denzil panting.

At last, the great wizard spoke again. "I think," he said, his voice quieter than ever, "that you had better pour me a cup of warm spiced wine. Then we will sit by the fire, you and I, and talk."

Sam heard Denzil cross the dusty floor; heard wine being poured, and the swish of heavy robes as the wizard reclined in his chair. There was a scuffle as Denzil sat on the warm hearthstones. Then, for a while, the only sounds in the room were the crackling of the fire in the grate and the whistle of the wind through the gaps between the shutters. Sam leaned against the stones of the ancient wall and waited for Denzil's story.

"Eight months ago," said Denzil, "I made a little mistake. I was dusting your books — the ones with the magic spells — and one accidentally fell open. I accidentally saw the words, and sort of — without really meaning to — kind of read them aloud. They just happened to be about going forward to Wednesday. And the next moment — well, after a wee while, maybe — I fell asleep, and when I woke up I was . . . well, in this other place. Sort of."

Valvasor was looking into the fire, and his eyes, narrowed to glowing slits, gave nothing away. He waited in silence for Denzil to go on.

Denzil swallowed nervously, then took a deep breath. "This other place was . . . well, it was a little bit ahead of us in time. A day or two. Seven hundred years, actually. I did a few things there, then came home. I'm sorry. I know I'm not allowed to look at your books, and I'm not supposed to work magic on my own. Not yet. It was a little mistake. Sorry."

"The books are not important," said Valvasor, still looking into the fire. "The day will come when you will know what is in those books as well as you know the pathways around your own home. What amazes me, Denzil, is the way your hand must have accidentally fallen on the key that unlocks my forbidden cupboard, and then, by a stroke of astounding good luck, just happened to touch the very thing you needed to make the spell work — the most sacred thing I own — the silver and gold talisman that holds the secret of Time. And all those fortuitous events worked together to make the most powerful magic of all — the passage across time and space, and back again. That is the most extraordinary series of accidents, and I can only presume that Destiny saw you worthy of them. And today I hear that an angel of God has come to give a blessing to you. So what right have I, who am only an ignorant wizard, to tell you that you are wrong?"

Denzil's mouth fell open. He stared, speechless, at his master's face, golden and glorious in the firelight. Valvasor looked very grave, but a small smile played about his lips.

Denzil gulped, and looked away. His heart pounded. So everything was all right then? No fit, no fury, no outraged ferocity? He was forgiven! Excused! Pardoned! He didn't have to worry, didn't need a witness to prove that he'd only borrowed the sacred charm, didn't have to get Sam to explain everything to . . .

Sam! Oh, gawd, thought Denzil, panic-stricken again. What do I do now, with Sam? But he noticed that Valvasor was watching his face closely, probably reading his mind, so he tried to look calm. But Sam wouldn't go out of his mind, and he was sure Valvasor knew about her. And if he knew, what would he do?

"It's time we thought about dinner," said Valvasor, standing up. "But it's too late to do a roast. We'll leave her in the stable for now, and in the morning we'll wring her neck and prepare her for cooking. She'll do for Christmas dinner."

Denzil flung himself at the wizard's feet.

"Oh, no, master! Not that!" he wailed. "She's my friend! She'll be quiet, I promise! She won't take up much room. She'll stay there with her lovely wings and all, and not be a bother. I swear it. Oh, have mercy, master! Mercy!"

"It's only a goose, Denzil!" said Valvasor, bewildered.

"Mother Goodhart didn't say she was giving it to you as a pet. She forgot to mention it, I suppose — she was so excited about seeing the angel. I thought she was giving us the bird for dinner. I had no idea you were so fond of it."

Denzil gave a relieved sigh, then stood up. Smiling, he tossed his tangled hair out of his eyes. "I'm not fond of it," he said. "I mean, I'll be even more fond of it when its neck's wrung and it's plucked and stuffed and smelling mighty fine over our fire."

Valvasor looked at him through narrowed eyes. "Sometimes, Denzil," he said, "you worry me." He opened a small pouch that hung from his leather belt, and gave Denzil a copper coin. "Go and buy some fresh bread from the baker's wife, and we'll make do with bread and cheese tonight."

Denzil raced out into the street. An owl flew out from under the thatch, and Denzil hooted at it. He ran on, bounding over the piles of snow, yelling and crowing, and sending the coin spinning in the misty evening air.

Valvasor smiled to himself and shook his head, then threw some more wood on the fire.

Hidden in the loft, Sam quietly stretched her cramped legs and hoped Denzil wouldn't forget she was there.

4 Request for an Angel

or ages Sam stayed in the loft, not daring to move, hardly daring even to breathe. She glanced down at her left wrist, and realised that she'd lost her watch. Dismayed, she hoped it wasn't out in the snow, getting ruined. She wondered what the time was, then realised that it didn't really matter. Who cared whether it was five o'clock or six o'clock, when you were already seven centuries late for dinner?

She felt Murgatroyd stretch and then start wriggling in her pocket, and she gently stroked him to keep him quiet. From the room below came sounds of plates being cleared away, and more wood being thrown on the fire. The house was in darkness, but on the far wall, above the huge wooden door with its black bolts, the firelight danced.

"Leave the plates and knives for now," Valvasor said. "It is snowing again, and dark, and you can wash the dishes in the river in the morning. I would speak with you awhile."

The plates stopped clattering, and Sam heard a chair scrape on the stone floor.

"I have a feeling," Valvasor began, "that there is something more you have to tell me, Denzil."

Denzil gulped nervously. "Not really, master," he said.

"Nothing? No more spells you just happened to mutter as you diligently dusted my books, no more magic accidentally whisking someone else through the curtains of Time?"

"N—no," squeaked Denzil.

Valvasor smiled, and stood up. "Then I can rest easy," he said. "'Tis my bedtime, Denzil. I have had a long day with much hard work in it. And a surprise or two. Blow out the candles before you go to sleep. And eat the last of that loaf of bread if you are still hungry."

High in the loft, Sam crept back into the blackness and lay very still. She was starving.

Don't eat the bread, Denzil, she thought, and her stomach rumbled so loudly that she was positive Valvasor would hear it. But the old wizard kicked off his shoes, removed his heavy outer robes, washed his face and hands in a bowl of water, and climbed into bed.

Denzil placed a thick fur beside the fire, spread several blankets over it, and climbed in. He took the bread with him.

"Little pig!" thought Sam, watching from above.

Angrily, and not very quietly, she wriggled back to the far wall, and wrapped her arms around her legs. Her dress itched, and she felt cold and tired. Cobwebs moved lightly on her hair when she leaned back, and she was sure the place was full of spiders. She could hardly see, it was so dark now, and the firelight had fallen to a dim glow in the room below. In the redness on the plastered wall she could see a painting of a cat. She remembered Murgatroyd, and put her hand into her pocket, thinking he might cheer her up. But her pocket was empty.

Carefully, she felt around the dim folds of her apron, and in the rougher folds of her skirt. She felt the wooden floor, disturbing dust two hundred years old, and touched a dried apple core, and something soft that felt like a fragment of fur. She quickly pulled away, and did not touch the floor with her hands again. She longed for a torch.

A black crow flew towards her out of the dimness, and she almost screamed, covering her face with her arms. There was a scuffling sound on the floor in front of her, and something grabbed her arm. She did begin to scream then, and a grubby hand was clapped across her mouth. She struggled, and her eyes flew open and stared into Denzil's face. He was furious.

"Stupid cow!" he hissed, removing his hand and peering over the edge of the loft at the wizard's bed.

Sam took a deep breath, and with trembling fingers picked up something that Denzil had thrown into her lap. She sniffed it; it was bread, fresh-baked and smelling delicious, and bumpy with grains.

"Thanks," she whispered, looking up. But only a snowy owl stood there, teetering on the edge of the loft, its great wings beating the black air. Dust flew across Sam, and she stifled a cough. The owl screeched, its wild cry sounding remarkably like Sam's scream, and soared off into the smoky ceiling. It landed on a beam not far away, and stared at Sam with smouldering and scolding eyes.

From below came impatient muttering, and a slipper sailed up through the air and nearly knocked the owl off its perch. The bird screeched again, flapping, then settled down and smoothed its ruffled feathers. It glared at the girl in the loft.

Sam covered her face with her hands and tried not to laugh. Below, Valvasor pulled the furs over his head, and soon started snoring. Sam ate the bread, nibbling it slowly to make it last. The owl roosted, its snowy feathers glimmering against the black beams. But its eyes weren't on Sam; they were staring hungrily at a white rat that crouched, quivering, on the top rung of the ladder. After a while the owl, with admirable self-control and a strong sense of having missed something savoury, stretched out its wings and sailed silently down to the room below. Looking over the edge of the loft, Sam glimpsed a small bottom in patched tights disappearing under a pile of blankets.

She crept to the back of the loft, found the fur rug,

and snuggled into it. A candle appeared on the floor by her head, and its flame comforted her.

At the top of the ladder the white rat washed its face and ears, and contemplated the mysteries and miracles of life among the feathered and the furred.

Denzil had grand plans, that night, of getting out of bed while Valvasor still snored, and looking up the spell necessary to send Sam home again.

But it was a bitter night; the wind whistled and wailed and rattled the shutters; icy gusts swept in under the door, lifting the mats and fur rugs on the floor, and blowing ash across the hearth; and snow came sliding down the chimney, to hiss and spit as it hit the hot embers. Denzil snuggled down into his furs and dozed.

Strange dreams he had, of hundreds of people crowding around him, cheering and yelling, while Valvasor turned him into a toad for telling lies; and then Rowl and the village boys put him in a cage and taunted him. They poked sticks at him, and swung the cage around until he was dizzy, and shook him until his eyes nearly fell out.

Then Denzil woke, but the dream went on, with people roaring and the shaking going on and on . . .

"Denzil! Wake up, lad!"

This time it was Valvasor who shook him, Valvasor who yelled, even louder than the crowd.

"Denzil! Wake up! The people want to see you."

37

Denzil sat up and rubbed his eyes. Valvasor was crouched near him by the hearth, his hand on Denzil's shoulder.

"The people wish to speak to you, Denzil. They wish to speak with the one who was visited by the angel yesterday. Quickly, get up and put on your best clothes, and wash the sleep from your face. Quickly — they've been waiting since dawn."

Bewildered, Denzil rolled out of the fur and plunged his shaking hands into the bowl of icy water. Shuddering, he splashed it on his face, then dried himself with the cloth the wizard handed him. Not daring to look at Valvasor, he scrambled into his best coat and pulled on his boots. Outside, the crowd still roared, calling for Denzil, the favoured one to whom God had sent an angelic messenger. Valvasor sat in the chair by the fire and watched, one eyebrow raised, an amused smile playing about his shrewd eyes.

At last Denzil stood before him, his hair roughly combed, his face shining. "I'm ready, master."

"Then go out and see them," said Valvasor, still smiling, as he settled down deeper into his chair.

Outside, the crowd grew frenzied, waiting to see the most honoured son in the whole village — probably in the whole kingdom.

"Won't you talk to them first, master?" asked Denzil, white-faced. "Just to settle them down a bit."

"But they don't want to see me," protested Valvasor. "They want to see you."

Denzil nodded gravely. With his heart pounding, he went over to the great wooden door. He hitched up his woollen hose, took a deep breath, and pulled back the bolt. The door swung open.

He was blinded by the sudden morning light, and a cheer like thunder broke across him. He stood blinking, his mouth hanging open.

Then, suddenly, the cheering stopped. Mother Goodhart came up to him, bowing low, her gaze lowered to the ground. She carried a basket full of gifts — winter berries, a small white fox-fur, and some sweet fruit pies, still steaming. There was a leather bottle of wine, some new knitted socks, a shirt woven of wool dyed in purple berry juice, and a new pair of shoes that the shoemaker had stayed up all night to make.

Mother Goodhart held the basket out to Denzil, though still she did not dare look into his eyes. Behind her, two hundred men, women, and children stood hushed. In the fields beyond, a flock of crows cracked the morning quiet with their raucous cries.

"Denzil, Apprentice to the great Valvasor," Mother Goodhart addressed him, "we of the village of Northwood give you this, as a sign of our great respect, since you are the angel's chosen one."

Denzil didn't move, so she put the basket on the ground in front of him. "And there's something else," she said, very softly. "Denzil, we need to see your angel."

Denzil's throat went dry, and he could feel his heart bouncing between his ribs. "*See* her?" he managed to croak.

Mother Goodhart nodded, and a murmur went through the crowd.

Mother Goodhart went on, earnestly, "This morning we have discovered sickness in our village. Sickness of the worst kind. It is the Black Death. Little Milda, the tailor's daughter, has it. If only your angel would come and see her, she would recover, and all will be well. Also, if your angel could bless our village, no one else would fall ill. We would all be saved."

She knelt before him, her eyes raised to his face now, pleading with him. Behind her stood all the people of Northwood: the mothers with babes whimpering in their arms and younger children clutching their skirts; the fathers with their sons standing at their sides, solemn and silent; and the steward from Sir Godric's manor-hall, his velvet robes splendid compared with the ragged garments of the village folk. And there were the boys and girls of Denzil's age, looking at him no longer with fear, but with desperate hope and a kind of awe.

Denzil stared at them all and licked his lips. He was shivering.

"The angel might not come," he said. "I can't just snap my fingers and whistle her up, you know."

"But you could pray," said a man, stepping forward.

"Aye — you could pray!" echoed the village folk.

Denzil nodded. He felt very tempted to disappear and not come back until after Christmas. "All right," he said. "I'll have a chat to God about it."

Smiling and murmuring their gratitude, the people went away. Denzil picked up the basket of gifts, went inside, and shut the door.

Valvasor was putting on his thick fur cloak and his leather boots, ready to go out. "I'll be away for the day," he said. "I'll leave you in peace to do your sacred work. Remember, Denzil, that people's lives hang on your prayers today. Pray well." Then he went out, leaving his apprentice to plead for the angel's return.

"Hey, Angel! Get down here!" yelled Denzil.

Valvasor flung open the door, and stared in astonishment.

"I heard that, Denzil," he said. "You shock me to my soul. That is no way to appeal to a heavenly being."

"Sorry," muttered Denzil, his face red. "I'll try again."

"With a little more respect," said Valvasor, and went out again.

For the benefit of the wizard in case he was still listening, Denzil called softly: "Sweet angel! I implore you, please come down and bless our humble village with your beauteous presence! I beg of you —"

Sam climbed down the ladder. "Put a sock in it, Denzil!" she said. "Things are bad enough already, without you standing there saying stupid things."

Denzil held his finger to his lips, and jerked his head

towards the door. They heard heavy footsteps walking away.

Denzil grabbed Sam's arm. "You've got to dress up again!" he said. "You've got to show yourself to the villagers."

"I can't! You heard what they said — little Milda's really sick. This has all gone too far, Denzil. Your magic's all out of control. I can't help little Milda — or anyone. I don't want to be an angel. I'm not going anywhere in your village. I'm going home." She crossed the room, took down a book of spells, and came back and put it firmly into Denzil's arms.

"Find the spell to send me home, please," she said.

Denzil glared at her over the book. "You'll get dressed in your angel's stuff, and go and see little Milda," he said.

"I will not. Look up that spell. Now!"

Denzil stuck out his chin, so Sam grabbed the book and started looking through it. With a howl of rage, Denzil grabbed it off her. "You can't read that!"

"I can so," said Sam. "I can read anything. I can definitely read your stupid old spells."

Denzil gulped. His face was white. "Please don't, Sam," he choked. "If you read these, anything could happen. And Valvasor would kill me."

"If you don't send me home right now," said Sam, "I'll knock your head off, and he won't have to."

Denzil bit his lower lip. Sam could hit pretty hard, as he remembered.

"Tell you what," he said. "We'll do a trade. You dress up as an angel and visit the folk and little Milda, and then I'll send you home."

"Straight away?" she said.

"Straight away."

"Promise?"

"Promise."

"Cross-your-heart-and-hope-to-die?" said Sam.

Denzil hesitated. "That's not a sensible thing to say," he said, "when there's Black Death in the village."

"What is Black Death, anyway?"

"Plague," he said. "You get the sneezes, and a sore throat, and red spots, and in three days you're dead."

"Blimey," said Sam. "It's serious then."

"Aye, it is," said Denzil.

Sam thought for a while, and at last she nodded.

"If it'll make people happy, I'll be an angel just one more time," she said. "But I can't really heal that little girl, Denzil. I probably shouldn't even go near her. I got chickenpox once, and none of my friends were allowed to visit me in case I gave it to them. Plague might be the same."

"It's very catching," said Denzil. "That's why the people want the angel to bless our village, so no one else gets sick."

"It's a pity you haven't got a real angel," said Sam, and Denzil nodded miserably.

"Sure would help," he said.

Sam put her arm about his shoulder. "I might as

43

well go and get my gear on," she said. "You'll have to undo the sewing down my back."

"Gawd, I just finished it!" groaned Denzil.

"If you're going to stand there grizzling," said Sam, removing her arm, "I'll read the spell myself, and go home."

"I'll help," said Denzil. "We'll go and get ready in the stable. There's a little door at the back of it that we shovel straw through in the summer. You can turn into an angel in there, and I'll gather all the village folk out behind the stable, where you first appeared. I'll get them all to face the west, away from the stable, and kneel down and pray. While they've got their eyes shut, you can crawl through the little door and stand up behind them. Then I'll make a flash of light, and cry out that you've come — and all the people will turn around and see you. It'll be marvellous!"

"It'll be better than the school play," said Sam, laughing, beginning to enjoy herself. "I'll even say the right lines and everything. Then you can send the people home, and we'll come back and you can look up the spell. It'll be easy. I'll be home before lunch."

5 The Visitation

t was dark and musty in the stable, and Denzil refused to light a candle in case the straw caught fire. But it was warm there, and a little daylight came in through the chinks in the wooden walls. After a great deal of difficulty and a few swear words, Denzil got the sewing unpicked down the back of Sam's dress. Though it was cold, she was glad of the smooth softness of her angel's gown. She kept the red stockings on underneath, and the medieval shoes. Then Denzil helped her on with her wings, and she told him how to tie the straps that secured them to her shoulders.

"They don't quite feel right," she said, cautiously moving her arms. "I hope they don't fall off."

"Just don't try to fly too high in them," said Denzil, and Sam pulled a face. He grinned. "They don't have to stay on for long," he said, "and you've only got to stand still. Anyway, if they start to fall off, I can cover you with light, and no one will see."

"I hope you know what you're doing," said Sam,

pushing her heavy curls out of her eyes. "I suppose I should do my hair if I'm supposed to look beautiful. Have you got a comb?"

"A comb?" said Denzil, looking blank again. "I haven't used that thing since the summer. Do you want me to look for it? It could be in my wooden chest in the house. Or in the chest with the spare furs, since I comb the fleas out of them with it. Or it could be here in the stable. Think I combed the donkey's tail, once —"

"Don't worry," said Sam, straightening her dress. "Now, where's that little door?"

"Behind the box with the straw in it," said Denzil. "Over there."

As Sam brushed past the long box full of straw, she heard a faint gurgling sound, and a soft cry. She looked down at the straw. It was dark, but a sliver of light from the back wall slanted across it. And in that light, wrapped in a ragged blanket, lay a baby.

"Denzil!" she gasped. "There's a baby here!"

Denzil came over, and leaned low over the straw. "Oh, Lord!" he groaned. "Not again!"

"What do you mean — not again?" cried Sam, horrified. "Do you find babies here all the time?"

Denzil smiled, and stuck his grubby finger in the baby's mouth. It suckled noisily, hungrily.

"Poor people sometimes bring their waifs to Valvasor if they haven't got enough food for them," he said. "He finds homes for them — gives them to people who can look after them, who won't leave them out in the snow to die."

"To die? Why would they do that?"

"Because sometimes the village folk get suspicious, they think a waif is a changeling. They kill changelings."

Sam's face was white. "What's a changeling?" she asked.

"A baby that's been swapped by the faery-folk for one of theirs. The faeries keep the human, and leave a changeling. It's usually a goblin; something awful. If the village folk thought it looked a bit weird, they'd call this little thing a changeling, and kill it. So its mother brought it here, to Valvasor. It's safe here. He doesn't mind changelings."

"But Valvasor's an old man," said Sam. "He doesn't know how to look after babies."

"He does so!" said Denzil fiercely. "I was a waif. And Valvasor kept me, and brought me up fine."

Sam stared at him, startled. She was about to ask him whether he'd been a changeling, since he looked a bit goblinish at times, but at that moment the stable door flew open and a man came in, calling for Denzil. Denzil swung around, trying to hide Sam and the waif. But it was too late. The man saw Sam. He came in slowly, squeezed past the donkey, and gazed at the angel with its white robes and beautiful wings. Slowly he took the hat from his head and knelt in the dirt. Three other men came in with him, crowding close in the dusty stable. They all saw Sam, and knelt.

"What's going on?" cried a woman's voice, from outside. "Is he there? Is Denzil there?"

"Aye — and the angel!" said a man.

A cold draft blew in, and, to Denzil's horror, the baby started to cry. "What's that?" cried a man, alarmed.

Denzil collapsed in the straw in front of the baby, and covered his face with his hands. "Oh, sweet Jesus!" he groaned.

There was a stunned silence. Then the men bent lower to the stable floor, their foreheads touching the dirt. Two women crept in, peering through the dimness.

"Sweet Jesus?" murmured one of the women, amazed. "By all the saints — 'tis the Christmas Child, born in Valvasor's own stable!"

"Can't be," said someone else behind her. "Not here in Northwood."

"It is," said the woman, crying, and kneeling down. "You heard Denzil — and you see the Holy Child, attended by an angel. Oh, our village is surely blessed above all the villages in our kingdom!"

The baby started to howl in earnest, and Denzil stared helplessly at Sam.

"Pick it up!" she hissed.

Awkwardly, he lifted the screeching bundle out of the straw and held it against his shoulder. It suckled into his neck, sounding like a little piglet, and Denzil grinned at the people bowed down on the stable floor.

"Guess I'd better take him in and feed him," he said. "You can all go home now."

"But the plague . . ." began a woman, in a low choking voice. "Just ask the angel to bless our village, and save us."

"We already is blessed," said a man, softly. "With the presence of the Christ Child hisself. Come home, Edyth. All's well."

They went out, crossing themselves, and sending long, awed looks back at the child in Denzil's arms, and the glowing angel that sheltered them.

When they were gone, Denzil turned to Sam. His face was one huge smile. "Couldn't have worked better, if the Good Lord Himself had organised it!" he said.

"Maybe He did," said Sam, just as her wings slid slowly down her back and sank majestically into a pile of donkey droppings.

Denzil heated some goat's milk over the fire, and Sam wrapped the screaming baby in a warm fur and tucked it carefully between the furs in Valvasor's bed.

"I'll feed it," she said, taking the bowl of warmed milk from Denzil. "You can read up the spell to send me home. Haven't you got a baby's bottle for the milk? I can't just pour the stuff in, even if the kid has got its mouth wide open."

"Use a rag," said Denzil, giving her a grey-looking piece of linen. "Dip it in the milk like this, see, and let the waif suck it."

Sam watched him admiringly. She didn't know he knew how to look after babies. He must have grown up a bit since she saw him last, even if he did smell again for want of a bath, and his hair hadn't been combed in six months.

"I wouldn't mind staying for a while," she said, taking the rag off him and dipping it in the milk again. "But I suppose I should go home. Mum's probably wondering where I am."

Denzil nodded, and went over to the books of spells. He tried very hard to look as if he knew what he was doing, but Sam noticed that he scratched his head often, and read through three books before he started copying something out. He wrote on a piece of stiff parchment, and used a quill dipped in ink. She could hear the quill scratching, and noticed that Denzil dripped more ink than he wrote with.

She finished feeding the baby and left it to snooze while she went and looked over Denzil's shoulder. He covered the spell with his arm.

"Don't read it," he said. "Not yet. If you read it before it's finished, you could end up splattered all the way between here and the twentieth century."

"Sounds messy," said Sam, shuddering. She was still wearing her angel dress, but had pulled the blue medieval one over the top. She still had on the red stockings and the soft leather shoes, but she felt very cold. And hungry. She went over to the shelf by the fire and looked at the food there. There was a mouldy cheese, a loaf of black bread, and some strange-looking little pies.

"What's in these?" she asked, pointing to the pies.

"Hedgehogs," said Denzil, and Sam pulled a face.

"Is there anything else to eat?" she asked.

"You could go and trap a rabbit," he said, dipping the quill in the ink again, and scribbling on the parchment.

Sam sat down in Valvasor's chair and told herself she wasn't hungry. Her stomach rumbled, and she felt slightly sick. She thought of potato chips and lemonade, and her mother's gingernuts. Suddenly she jumped up.

"I can't go back, not yet!" she cried. "I've lost Murgatroyd! I can't go back without him! And I've lost my watch too, the Mickey Mouse one Grandad gave me. I've got to find them."

"Mickey Mouse?" said Denzil, frowning. "Who's he? A friend of Murgatroyd's?"

"I'll go and look outside," said Sam. "And then we'll look in the loft for Murgatroyd. He must still be up there, somewhere."

"I'll finish writing this out," said Denzil, "and then, if you don't find your critters, I'll turn myself into an owl, and find them in no time. There's nothing to worry about, Sam. Honest."

Sam didn't look so sure. She went outside, all along the tracks in the snow to the stable, to the back of the stable where she had arrived yesterday, and back to the house again. Denzil was still writing the spell, so she climbed the ladder to the loft, and, in the grey daylight, looked for her bright red watch and Murgatroyd.

She found neither.

She was about to go back down the ladder again when the front door flew open, and in swept a bent, stormy-looking figure like a scarecrow, all ragged clothes and wild grey hair and a face like a frenzied chicken. The individual even sounded like a chicken, clucking and muttering about the terrible winter and the mud and slush, while it flapped across the floor to the fire.

Sam leaned over the edge of the loft and stared, eyes wide with astonishment. The stranger dropped a red shawl, peeled off a black cape, and kicked her pair of muddy long-toed boots clear across the room. Then she bent over with her bottom to the fire, slowly raised two long skirts and four petticoats, and groaned in ecstasy as the warmth seeped through her britches.

Sam got the giggles, but fortunately the visitor didn't hear. She began to do an odd little dance in front of the fire, turning and dipping, and pointing first one foot and then another to the fire, and then bending over and warming her bottom again. All the time she muttered and clicked her tongue. With her beaky nose, bright black eyes, and skinny legs in red stockings sticking out of feather-white petticoats, she looked exactly like an excited chicken. She was ancient, lively, and utterly fantastic. And while she pranced and fluttered, Sam was sure music played — jaunty, joyous music of pipes and flutes. Sam was enchanted.

Denzil was not. He put down his quill, pushed back his chair, and shouted angrily: "Valvasor didn't say you were coming."

The music stopped. The old woman froze in the middle of her dance, one toe lifted towards the fire, her beady eyes half-closed as she listened. Her incredibly wrinkled face was screwed up in bewilderment.

"Mother Wyse!" shouted Denzil. "I didn't know you were coming!"

Mother Wyse dropped her petticoats, smoothed down her crumpled skirts, and slowly turned around. "There is no crow in my plumbing," she said, with great dignity. "There may be a lot of mud and leaves about, but I always clear out that little drain down to the stream. You have no business criticising my toilet arrangements. Now tell me, where is Valvasor?" .

"Out," said Denzil.

Mother Wyse clucked and muttered again. "A pity. A great pity, that. It's not wise, to turn himself into a trout this time of year. The streams are frozen over. When will he be back?"

"When he comes in the door," said Denzil.

"When he's swum in the thaw? He's waiting until springtime?" cried Mother Wyse, horrified. She took a few deep breaths to calm herself. "Oh well, he has to, I suppose. Can't jump out of water that's all frozen over. It's a long time to leave you alone though. Perhaps I should move in here and look after you. Yes. Yes, that's what I'll do. I'll whisk all my books and animals and things over here, and we can all settle in nicely until springtime. Now, what's the spell for transmitting —"

"No! No, don't!" howled Denzil. "I'm all right! Valvasor's coming back soon. Today. This very hour, maybe."

"Coming down in the next shower?" asked Mother Wyse. "But I thought you said he was a trout. Did you mean a waterspout?"

Denzil groaned. "He's not a trout, or a waterspout!" he shouted.

"He's not?" said Mother Wyse. "Then why did you say he was? You have a wicked sense of humour at times, Weasel. Valvasor trusts you a great deal, with all this wondrous magic he's teaching you. I hope you are worthy of it."

"I am," said Denzil, his green eyes flashing angrily. "And I'm Denzil, not Weasel."

"All right. No need to get frazzled, even if you are feeble. You don't show your elders enough respect."

"I do! I respected you! I trusted you! I told you all about the galaxy and the dragon called Trayne! I told you my best secrets. And you went and told Valvasor! Now I'm in the biggest pickle I've ever been in, and it's all your fault!"

"Biggest prickle?" said Mother Wyse, frowning. "In your foot? Come here, and I'll dig it out. Valvasor's got a knife somewhere, hasn't he?"

Denzil shot around to the far side of the table, wailing.

"You really can't look after yourself, Weasel," murmured Mother Wyse. "I'll just bring a few things over, and everything will be all right. Stop fussing, dearie. I've got a little knife of my own that will do quite nicely for your prickle."

She stood very still in the centre of the room and chanted in a low and solemn voice:

"Hams and herbs and hives of bees,
Pots and pans and pickled cheese,
Leeks and linen, leather shoes,
Jars of brains and secret brews,
Eggs and kegs of yellow whey,
All that's vital for my stay,
Broomstick, cauldron, cool black cat,
Spinning-wheel and stunning hat —
Transport here, before me, now!
(And don't forget my Jersey cow!)"

"No!" yelled Denzil.

It was too late. There was a tremendous crash, and the whole house shook. Dust exploded everywhere, mud rained, and clods of earth shot through the air like missiles. Slowly the dirt settled, and out of the dust and turmoil appeared Mother Wyse's cottage, plonked in the middle of Valvasor's polished floor.

Luckily her cottage was small, but even so the thatched roof touched the rafters. Dust poured out of the cracks in the walls, and rose through chinks in the roof. And all around were clumps of earth and bits of broken stone that had fallen off in the upheaval. Bees buzzed angrily in the haze, and a dazed cow stared nervously at Denzil, and belched loudly.

Slowly the front door of the cottage creaked open, and Mother Wyse staggered out in a cloud of smoke and dust.

"Well, that's one way to rearrange the furniture," she said cheerfully. "Could you come in and help me, Weasel? There's a wee bit of a mess in here."

Denzil shook his head, and dirt and grit slid down him onto the floor. He could hear Sam laughing up in the loft, but he wasn't laughing himself. His face was a motley shade of red, and Mother Wyse suspected he wasn't thrilled with the situation.

"It's for your own good, Weasel," she said. "We'll both be quite comfortable here, as soon as I sweep up my garden. Now, what's happened to my broom?"

"I'll tell you what's going to happen to it, and to everything else," said Denzil, spitting dirt. "It's all going back."

"It is *not* going to be ransacked," said Mother Wyse. "It's in a big enough shambles already."

"I said, *it's going back!*" shouted Denzil.

"I suppose it *is* sagging backwards a smidgen," said Mother Wyse, with a worried frown. "Sagging a bit in all directions, actually. Can you remember that spell for fortifying walls? Or was it for glorifying halls? You know, it was something about edifice and hardness and . . ."

"And homeless and brainless, by the time I've finished," muttered Denzil. A roguish gleam came into his eyes. And before Mother Wyse could say another word, he started chanting:

"Wipe it,
Swipe it,
Stick it back and right it!
Get it out of my place,
Set it out of my space!
Disappear
Out of here
NOW!"

From her perch in the loft, Sam saw the strangest thing. It was the opposite of the huge explosion of before: this time there were clouds of dust and earth and grass, but instead of all rumbling outwards, they all rolled inwards, becoming smaller and more intense, mud and dirt and ancient stone gathering inwards, shrinking, until all was gone.

But not quite all. The cow still stood there, chewing a tuft of grass and staring in a bewildered way at the space where the cottage had been. It looked annoyed at being left behind. Mother Wyse stood beside the cow, and Denzil couldn't tell whether the old woman was annoyed or not. Neither did he care.

He sat down at the table again, brushed some grit off the parchment, and picked up the quill, stabbing it so hard into the ink that the end buckled. When he tried writing, the quill wobbled dangerously across the magic-laden words.

Mother Wyse watched him, then said quietly:

"And now undo
What's been undone,
His spell outdo,
Make mine the one
That rules the stones
And rules the thatch,
That settles zones
And sets the patch."

In another eruption of dust and shattered earth, the cottage arrived. The cow, definitely upset now, flared its nostrils dangerously. Mother Wyse scratched her whiskery chin, peered at Denzil through the dust, and cackled triumphantly.

Denzil didn't even blink. But he stopped writing just long enough to say:

"Mine the magic,
Mine the skill
Mine the logic
To now fulfil
My dream for this,
Your misplaced space,
Which I dismiss
To yonder place!"

With a rattle and a roar, the cottage was off again. This time even the cow went, and they heard her mooing in the distance, indignantly.

Mother Wyse stood shaking for a while, staring hard at Denzil. He bent his head over the parchment again, his lips curved.

"I think I'll begin this visit again," murmured Mother Wyse. She walked slowly over to the door and knocked on it. "Good day to you, Weasel! Is Valvasor home?" she called.

"I hope not," said Denzil. "He'd be flattened by now."

"Flattered? To see me?" she said, looking pleased. "Kind of you to say so, Weasel. Actually, I came to invite you both to a Christmas feast at my house . . . ah, if my house is still there, that is. We will have roasted goose, potatoes baked in the ashes, and cabbage boiled in my cauldron. And especially for you, honey and hedgehog pie. Possibly with dust in it."

"Thank you, Mother," said Denzil. "That would be very nice."

"Good," said Mother Wyse. "And I'm very pleased to see that your magic is progressing so quickly. Very rapidly, in fact. Watching you at work was quite a moving experience."

"Thank you," said Denzil, with the sweetest smile.

Mother Wyse went and picked up her boots, her shawl and cape, and put them all on. Then, without another word, she left.

6 Rat Hunt!

Before Sam had a chance to climb down the ladder, the front door burst open again and Valvasor came in.

Denzil looked up from the spell, his face scarlet with guilt. But Valvasor didn't even notice what Denzil was doing. The wizard strode over to the fire, stood with his hands stretched out to the flames, and said solemnly: "We are in mortal danger, Denzil."

Denzil slid the quill and ink into a drawer in the huge table, quietly closed the book, and put it away. The parchment he rolled and slipped down his shirt.

"I know we are," Denzil said. "Mother Wyse is a terrible cook. I suppose you saw her, just before you came in."

"I did," said Valvasor, "but she was flying over Mother Gurtler's roof, and choking in the smoke. She's getting too old for flying — won't go high enough. But I wasn't talking of her when I said we were in mortal danger. It's not only you and I in danger, Denzil; it is our entire village. There is plague among us. I have seen the child. The red blotches are already upon her, and death cannot be far away."

"I know, master," said Denzil. "That's why the villagers wanted to see the angel. To ask for protection."

"And that is a good and right thing to do," said Valvasor. "But there is other work too, that we can do to protect ourselves. I've been talking to the mole-catcher and his son. They are arranging a rat hunt. That will at least ensure that plague-bearing fleas will not be carried by the rodents to other villages. You and I will help in the rat hunt. I will turn us into owls, and we will catch them naturally."

"A rat hunt?" asked Denzil, white-faced. "What will they do with all the rats?"

"Burn them," replied Valvasor. "They carry plague. By this time tomorrow, not one rat will remain in Northwood alive."

Denzil shook his head wildly, and wailed something about Murgatroyd.

At the same time there was a sound from the loft above; a strangled cry, full of anguish. Valvasor glanced up, his black eyes narrowed and searching.

But then a louder sound came from his bed — a long, quivering whimper that wound itself gradually up into a full-throated howl. Relieved, Denzil noticed Valvasor look at the bed. A puzzled frown crossed the elderly wizard's face.

"We've got a waif," Denzil announced. "It was in the stable."

Valvasor gave his apprentice a long, hard stare. "Have you any more surprises hidden away?" he asked. "If so, you'd better give them to me now."

Denzil swallowed nervously. "Actually, there is one," he confessed. "Her name's — "

But before he could say another word, there was a hammering at the door, and the sound of excited voices.

The door opened, and Denzil glimpsed a whole crowd of people, all wrapped well in winter rags, and holding pitchforks, sticks, nets, brooms, and other deadly weapons. But only two people came in to talk to Valvasor — Swifty the mole-catcher, and his son Rowl.

Rowl, looking proud and self-important, stared at Denzil and did not greet him. Denzil stared back, and noticed the club tied to Rowl's leather belt, and the bag to carry dead rats in. The bag was empty now, but in a few hours it would be bulging with brown and bloodied bodies.

"I've given the village folk their instructions, just as you said," Swifty told Valvasor. "We'll start the hunt at the mill-pond end of the village, going through the fields and farms. Then we'll work our way through the village, checking all the houses, stables, huts, and sheds. Not one rat will escape."

"The women will go first, beating drums," said Rowl eagerly. "They'll scare the rats out of their holes.

Then, while they're running along the ground looking for new hiding-places — WHAM! — we'll squash 'em with our brooms, stick 'em through with our pitchforks, slice off their little feet — "

"We can't!" howled Denzil, and they all looked at him, surprised.

"You've killed rats before, lad," said Valvasor gently, looking enquiringly at his apprentice. "Why the change of heart?"

"Because he's cowardly," said Rowl, with a slow smile. "He's a chicken-livered milksop."

Denzil went bright red, and Swifty gave his son a kick in the backside. Rowl stumbled forward a little way, but he didn't stop smirking. There was an awkward silence.

Then Swifty said to Denzil, a little angrily: "What's the matter with you, boy? Do you want those filthy little plague-bearing beasts to spread, and kill us all?"

Denzil's tongue stuck to the roof of his mouth. He could hardly say that one of those filthy beasts went under the grand title of Murgatroyd, and was brought here by the very angel who was supposed to save them all. Just then a terrible thought struck Denzil — a thought so appalling and disastrous that he almost fainted at the shock of it.

"Well, you go and begin your work," said Valvasor, putting his arm on Swifty's elbow and leading him to the door. "I have to visit someone, then I'll do my share of rat-catching. So will my apprentice."

63

Swifty and Rowl went out, and there were sounds outside of a great many people talking excitedly and organising themselves. Soon drums began to beat, and there was a roar of savage joy. The villagers loved a good hunt.

Denzil listened, his face growing pale as parchment.

Valvasor put on heavy boots and his thick fur cloak, all the time looking sideways at his apprentice. After a while he went over to Denzil and put his hand on the boy's shoulder.

"Is there anything you want to tell me, son?" he asked softly. "Are you in trouble?"

Denzil shook his head and said nothing.

"I'm visiting the sick child, to give her medicines," said Valvasor. "I shall be back in an hour. If the waif should waken, please give it more milk." He glanced once more at Denzil's frightened face, and went out.

The door had hardly banged shut behind him when Sam slithered down the ladder, rushed over to Denzil, and gripped him by the shirt.

"What are you going to do now?" she cried. "You'd better find Murgatroyd, and find him fast. I want him back in one piece, Denzil. I want him whole, unsquashed, alive, with no holes in him, and all his feet on. Find him. Now. Before that Rowl does."

Denzil just looked at her, and his green eyes, up close, seemed unusually big and full of fear.

"Sam," he choked, "I've just thought of something awful."

"What?" she said. "Do you have to have a bath tonight?"

"No. Sam, what if . . . What if it was Murgatroyd who brought plague to our village? We've never had plague before. And suddenly it's here. And so is Murgatroyd."

"Murgatroyd hasn't brought plague," she said. "We don't have plague where I live. Anyway, Dad and I checked him over carefully just last week, after my cat accidentally got hold of him. He was fine."

"I suppose he would have died," said Denzil, "if he'd bitten a rat with plague."

"I didn't mean my cat!" said Sam. "Murgatroyd was fine. I saved him before he got hurt. He's a very healthy rat, Dad says. Even if he is too well fed, and a bit fat."

"He'll make a big mess when they squash him," said Denzil gloomily. Sam shook him by the shirt. "Find him!" she hissed. "And find him *fast*."

Haughtily, with as much dignity as he could manage, Denzil pulled free from her grip, straightened his shirt and hitched up his hose.

"I'll find him easily," he said. "I have a plan."

"It'd better be a good one," said Sam, hearing the throb of drums and the shouts of excited people far in the distance. "I want Murgatroyd, and my watch, and I want that spell to send me home. I want them now. You've got five minutes."

Denzil didn't know what five minutes were, but he

guessed she wouldn't wait until after Christmas. He cleared his throat and tried to look calm and unruffled.

"This is the plan," he said. "I'm going to turn myself into a rat and sniff Murgatroyd out. I'll find him before you can blink."

"Oh, that's a brilliant idea!" scoffed Sam, furious. "Then I'll have two squashed friends, and no one to get me back home! Think of something else. Quick!"

"You think of something!" cried Denzil. "You're the one who's caused all the trouble."

"*Me?* What have I done? I was standing on my back lawn at home having my photo taken. You were the one who got me into this mess!"

"No I wasn't! You said the magic words, too! And it wasn't me wearing angel clothes and pretending to be all high and mighty!"

"I wasn't pretending anything! I'd be home doing our Christmas play now, if you hadn't messed things up with your stupid spells!"

"They're not stupid! You say that once more, and I'll change you into a frog and throw you in the duck pond!"

"You dare! Go on — try it!" Sam's fists were up, and she looked mad enough to knock Denzil's head off.

"Colour green, with slimy sheen —" began Denzil, but the baby woke up and started screaming. Sam picked it up, and told Denzil to heat up some more milk.

Denzil bent over the cauldron, and the frog spell got lost in smoky mutterings about bossy girls. Sam sat in Valvasor's chair and rocked the howling baby in her arms. She sniffed, and lifted the agitated bundle off her lap.

"Yuk! The baby's all wet," she said loudly, over the noise. "Have you got any nappies?"

"Any what?" asked Denzil, dipping a bowl in the warm milk and setting it on the hearth.

"You know . . . britches for the baby."

Denzil shrugged. "I don't know what Valvasor used," he said. "Nothing good, that's for sure, because the brats kept wetting them."

Sam gave the baby to Denzil, and went over to the wooden chest beside Valvasor's bed. She lifted the lid and started looking through the clothes.

"You shouldn't do that," said Denzil uneasily. "He keeps his ceremonial stuff in there. If you mess it up, he'll know."

Sam lifted out a shimmering piece of rainbow-coloured silk, and draped it over the edge of the chest. "Nice," she said, "but it's a bit slippery."

She delved deep in the chest, and noticed the smell of wild herbs that the wizard used to keep out mice and moths. At last she found a soft square of white material that she thought would do. She went back to the baby, took it off Denzil, and lay it on the fur by the fire to change it. Denzil went back to the book of spells, and tried to look knowledgeable. And all the

67

time the banging of drums came nearer, and the savage shouts of people after blood.

Quickly, Sam wrapped the white cloth around the baby since there weren't any safety pins to do the job properly, and started to give the child the milk. She glanced uneasily at Denzil.

"You're supposed to be finding Murgatroyd," she said.

Denzil bit his nails and said nothing.

"Hurry up!" shouted Sam, and the baby choked in fright. The drums were coming closer.

Sam finished feeding the baby, put it in Valvasor's bed again, and went over to Denzil. He was leaning over a well-worn page, reading earnestly.

"What are you looking for?" she asked.

Denzil mumbled something she couldn't hear. He was looking pale and nervous, and his face was sweating. Sam got the feeling that he wasn't exactly in control of the situation.

"I suppose," she said, "I could be an angel again, and tell the village folk that it's wrong to kill the rats."

"They won't believe you," said Denzil. "Rats have caused plague for hundreds of years."

"They've got to be stopped, Denzil! If they kill Murgatroyd . . ."

"All right," he said desperately. "I'll stop them. I'll turn all the rats into something people can't hurt."

"Like what?"

"I don't know. Balls of wool."

"Oh, great! And I'll get Murgatroyd back all stretched out and knitted into socks!"

"Clay, then! I'll turn all the rats into clay! Then all we have to do is look for a white lump of clay, and we've got Murgatroyd back!"

"That's no good!" howled Sam. "What if someone makes something out of him, and I get him back looking like a vase, with flowers stuck up his tail? Stones would be better, then no one could mess him up."

"Stones!" cried Denzil, green eyes ablaze. In his excitement, he jumped up and almost hugged Sam. Then he turned to the book again, and frantically turned the pages.

"Here it is!" he yelled. " 'Spell to Turn Living Things to Stone.' "

He read to himself for a while, muttering, and chewing his lower lip. Sam waited, and all the time the shouting and drums sounded louder and more terrible. "Hurry!" she cried, almost in tears.

"I've got it," said Denzil at last. "But I've got to hold a bit of fur in my hand and have a stone under my foot while I say it. I'll get a stone. You get some fur."

He dashed outside, and Sam went to the shelf near the fireplace and took down a lethal-looking knife. She crouched by one of the fur rugs on the floor, and sliced off a corner. Denzil ran in again, puffing, and grabbed the fur off her. He calmed himself down a bit, closed his eyes, and said:

69

"Fur and teeth and blood and bone,
Things that squeak and run alone,
Eye and beak and all that's flown,
Things that peek and shriek and moan,
Life that's born and breathed and grown —
Forget the careworn days you've known,
Sleep awhile, your life postpone,
Deep, immobile, safe in stone."

7 Meeting Emmeline

or a few moments Denzil and Sam stood perfectly still, waiting, listening, their breaths held. It was as if for a few seconds all life stood still. Even the frenzied sounds outside were stilled. Then they went on again, and life breathed once more.

"Reckon I did it," said Denzil grinning, and he ran outside. But something fell out of the sky onto his head and he stumbled dizzily about, yelling in pain and anger. He picked the thing up.

"What is it?" asked Sam, from the doorway behind him.

"A stone," said Denzil, going back and handing it to her.

"It's warm," she said, dropping it, and watching it melt a round patch in the snow. "And a funny brown colour. What is it, Denzil?"

"A sparrow, I think," he said. "I read the spell in a hurry, and didn't notice it was for birds as well."

Sam stared at him, horrified. "For rats *and* birds?"

71

she said. "And everything else with fur and feathers, I suppose."

Denzil went a bit red, and grinned sheepishly. "Well, nothing can come to any harm," he said. "Come on. We'll go and look for a white stone. We'll try the stable first."

"Then you'll turn the stone back into Murgatroyd?" she asked. "And everything else back into what it was before?"

"I don't have to," said Denzil. "The spell undoes itself, after a while."

"What kind of a while?" Sam asked.

"The short kind, I hope," said Denzil, and hurried off to the stable. But there was no white stone in the stables. There was a large grey stone that would have been the donkey, a pale one that would have been the goose, and many little brown ones like the sparrow.

"Don't worry," said Denzil cheerfully, heading off outside again. "We'll just start searching the houses. Everyone's still out looking for rats."

"They're not," said Sam, anxiously. "Listen. The drums have stopped, and everyone's quiet."

"They're probably wondering what all the stones are," said Denzil, giggling. "Maybe they've been hit on the heads by falling sparrows." He looked worried, momentarily. "Gawd. I hope there weren't any great eagles flying around up there. One of those could give someone an awful headache."

He disappeared into a shadowy thatched hut, and

Sam ducked her head under the low door and followed him.

It was very dark inside, for the windows were few and tiny and closed with shutters to keep out the cold. Sam was relieved to find no one at home, though the fire in the pit in the middle of the floor was still burning, and the room was full of smoke. Some of the fumes disappeared out holes at either end of the high thatched roof, and fish and pieces of bacon hung in the rafters, drying in the smoky heat. There were onions and leeks hanging on the walls, and in one corner was a stone oven. The fire in it had almost gone out, and there was a round loaf of bread baking on the hot ashes.

On a rough trestle table sat several strange kegs made of wood. One contained a huge lump of smelly cheese, while others were full of whitish liquid. Sam leaned over a keg, sniffed, and retched. She stepped back, covering her nose with her hand.

Behind her on the trampled dirt floor was a tall, narrow wooden vessel with a closed top. A handle poked out of the top, and Sam gave it a twirl. There was a thick liquid inside. "What's this?" she asked.

"A butter churn," Denzil replied. He picked up one of the small kegs and drank some of the liquid. He licked his lips, and gave a satisfied sigh.

"Yuk!" cried Sam, disgusted. "How can you drink that stuff? It stinks!"

"No it doesn't. It's whey. It's what we press out of

the cheeses. We have to make everything ourselves, here. It's not like your place, with a marvellous fair just down the street."

Sam looked away, vowing that she'd never again complain about going to the shop.

Denzil laughed, put down the container of whey, and poked his fingers in the cheese. "No rats have been gnawing this," he said. "Well, don't stand gawking. Look around for a white stone."

Sam climbed a rickety ladder to a loft at the far end of the room. The loft was piled with hay, and the smoke up there was so thick she could hardly see, or breathe. The loft formed a ceiling for a short passage leading to the yard outside. On the other side of the loft, and separated from the kitchen and living space by the passage, was another room. Looking down, Sam noticed more hay, and wondered whether this other room was where the people slept. Then she noticed two large pale rocks on the dirt floor, and screamed.

"The people!" she cried. "You've turned *people* into stones!"

Denzil dropped the hot bread he was devouring. White-faced, he climbed the ladder to the loft.

"Where?" he choked, frantically looking around. "Where are they?"

"Down there," said Sam, pointing to the rocks on the floor of the other room below. "Two people. You've really done it this time, Denzil."

"Down there?" asked Denzil, peering over the edge

74

of the loft. Suddenly he sat back on his heels. "Stupid cow!" he yelled. "What'd you go and frighten me like that, for? Those aren't people! Those are Master Gurtler's oxen! That's his stable, you fool!"

"His stable?" cried Sam. "His oxen? In the *house?*"

"Why not?" snarled Denzil, climbing back down the ladder again, and going outside. "Everyone keeps their oxen in the house. Gawd, you're dumb!"

Sam followed him out, and they stood blinking in the sudden bright light. Sam shivered. The small cobblestone courtyard was white with snow, and snow lay on the tops of the wobbly wooden fences surrounding the vegetable garden and the small piggery. There were tiny round buildings in the yard, thatched with straw like the house. Denzil went over to them, crouched down, and searched inside for something. He came back to Sam, two speckled stones in his hand.

"Hens," he said. "I did a good job, did I not?"

"We'll know that," she said, "when we've found Murgatroyd."

Denzil shot her a haughty look, and went off to inspect the other buildings in the yard. There was a low wooden shed on the other side of a haystack, with several white stones outside, too large to be Murgatroyd. Sam touched one with her foot, and wondered what kind of animal it had been.

"It was a goat," said Denzil.

She followed him across the cobblestones, stepping

carefully over the frosty straw and the animal droppings. The stones were slippery with ice, and the place stank of animals and rubbish. Across a broken wooden fence were other houses, all of them small like this one, and with their own vegetable gardens and animal houses. There were carts in some back yards, and barrels to collect rainwater. The whole village was tiny, the dirt streets narrow, the buildings small and dingy. Though the winter wind was sharp, the village reeked of smoke, cooking smells, and animals. And it was deathly quiet and still.

"I don't like this," said Sam, treading on a small pink stone, and apologising to it.

"Don't like what?" asked Denzil.

"Everything turned to stone. It's not nice."

"Murgatroyd wouldn't be nice either, squashed flat with his gizzard and eyeballs busting out," said Denzil.

Sam started to say something else, but a furious little woman came rushing around a corner, brandishing a straw broom. She rushed at Denzil, hitting him over the head and making straw fly everywhere.

"Out!" screamed the woman, shaking the broom. "Out, you wicked little thief!" She swiped at Denzil again, and he leapt away, laughing, until the broom caught him across the backside, and he yelped and started sprinting in earnest.

"Someone's already stole my hens!" shrieked the woman, as Denzil hurdled over the fence into the street. "I won't have my bread stole, as well!"

"I wasn't after your bread, Mother Gurtler!" yelled back Denzil. "It's not nice, anyway — you put beans in it. Besides, I'm a burglar, not a thief!"

He ran like a hare down the frozen road, did a magnificent skid on the ice, and ended up crashing into a cart someone had abandoned, with a black rock instead of a horse in the halter.

Sam had been so astounded at Mother Gurtler's fury and Denzil's cheek that she had remained perfectly still, half hidden behind a tall barrel that collected Mother Gurtler's rainwater. But the woman saw Sam, and stopped and squinted at her.

"Haven't I seen you before?" Mother Gurtler asked.

Sam had a sudden recollection of women and men kneeling in Valvasor's stable before an angel and a child.

"No," Sam replied. "I'm new here."

Mother Gurtler shook her head and clucked like a bewildered hen. "Seen you somewhere, I have," she said. "Anyway, child, don't play with that Denzil lad, if you want to stay out of trouble. Beware — he's a strange one."

"I know," said Sam, smiling.

She followed Denzil up the dirt road, and he looked in some houses while she looked in others. Sam was saddened at the poverty of the village, at the dirt and destitution in the tumbledown homes. And she felt like a thief, poking about in the few belongings the people did have. She found several small stones, probably mice, but no white stone that could have been Murgatroyd.

Feeling depressed, she bent her head and entered the last home to be searched. As she straightened up from the low doorway, she noticed that someone was there. It was a girl of about fifteen, sitting on a low stool by the fire. She held a piece of wood in her hands, and a small sharp knife. Fragments of wood shavings littered her grubby grey apron, and Sam noticed that she was carving the wood into a shape.

"Who is there?" asked the girl, though she looked directly at the place where Sam stood. Sam saw that the girl's eyes were a pale blue, so light that they had almost no colour at all.

"I'm a friend of Denzil's," said Sam. "I'm sorry. I didn't know anyone was home. I'm looking for a ra— for a white stone. A special one."

"I have no stones here," said the girl. Her hair was long and very dark, and her face, though grimy with soot, was beautiful. There was something serene about the way she sat with her hands so still in her lap, and her face uplifted and faintly smiling. She seemed very happy, though Sam couldn't understand why.

"I'm sorry I bothered you," said Sam, turning to leave.

"You have not disturbed me," said the girl, smiling at the air above Sam's head. "I have just this moment finished what I was making."

"What is it?" asked Sam, crossing the dirt floor.

"A fox," said the girl, holding the carving out towards Sam.

Sam took the carving out of the girl's hand. It was a wonderful fox, with a bushy tail held high and proud, and a face full of cleverness and a wild kind of laughter.

"How do you know what they look like?" asked Sam, astounded.

"I play with the little foxes sometimes, out in the summer fields," replied the girl. "Animals have no fear of me. But the villagers kill them if they catch them, because they damage the crops."

"It's a beautiful fox," said Sam, handing it back.

The girl pushed the carving back into Sam's hand, and closed Sam's fingers around it. "Keep it," she said. "I think you love animals too, since you are not out hunting the rats with all the other folk."

"Are you sure I can have it?" asked Sam.

"I am sure. I will make another. That is all I have to do; carve animals from wood."

"You do excellent carving," said Sam, "especially considering . . ."

"I can feel the shape of the little foxes in the fields," said the girl, "and I can feel the wood, and the shape I form it in. I work by touch."

"You're very clever," said Sam. "Thank you for the fox. I'll keep it always."

The girl smiled, her strange pale eyes not quite on

Sam's face. She was blinking a little, because a strand of hair had fallen across her eyes, irritating them. Without thinking, Sam bent down and gently brushed the hair away.

"Thank you," said the girl, and Sam turned and quickly went outside, the little wooden fox warm in her hand.

Denzil was waiting for her. As they walked past the vegetable garden to the village road, he said: "I heard you talking to Emmeline. I forgot she'd still be here. Did you frighten her?"

"I don't think so," said Sam. "She looks so peaceful, I think nothing would ever frighten her. She gave me this."

She showed Denzil the fox, and he grinned. "Clever, she is," he said. "If she carves like that when she's blind, imagine what she could do if she could see."

They looked in a few other hen houses and gardens along the way, then noticed that the people were coming back to their homes, carrying their pitchforks and clubs, and the terrible sacks of bloodied rats.

Sam eyed the sacks anxiously. "You don't think they got him, do you?" she whispered. "They could have got him before you made the spell."

"No. He'll be all right," said Denzil brightly, but he slipped his hand briefly into Sam's, and squeezed it. "We'll look in the mill, and in the bake house. The mill's always got rats; they like the grain and flour."

At that moment Rowl, the mole-catcher's son, came

along the road and saw them. Rowl was swinging a
blood-stained club from his right hand, and from his
left hand swung a bulging sack.

8 Black Wings and White Wings

s that your sweet maid, Denzil?" asked Rowl, grinning, as Denzil let go Sam's hand.

Sam glanced at Denzil. He looked red and angry, but he didn't say anything. He just nudged Sam with his elbow, and tried to walk past Rowl.

But Rowl kept moving sideways, preventing them from going past. All the time Rowl had a nasty grin on his face, and he swung the full sack so it brushed Sam's skirt and made her shiver.

"She's a timid little wench, isn't she?" said Rowl, swinging the sack close to Sam's face, and laughing when she ducked away. "Would you like to see all my squashed rats? I've got brown ones and black ones and grey ones and big ones and little tiny baby ones. You'd love the baby ones."

"Shut up," said Sam.

"Oooh, she's got a tongue in her head," said Rowl,

looking surprised. "Got a crabby look about her, too. I'd watch her, Denzil. She's got a frown mean enough to make the milk go sour. She'd mess up your spells, too, if you weren't careful. Come to think of it, she looks like a little witch. Still, I suppose a witch suits a wizard. Did she put a spell on you, to make you fall in love? You're such a weak little milksop, you wouldn't stand a chance."

Denzil looked terribly angry, but he didn't say a word. He was trying very hard not to turn Rowl into something little and squashable. Denzil had made a promise to Valvasor that he would never use his powers to hurt another human being in any way, or to change their shape against their will. It was a solemn promise, and Denzil would never break it. But at times like this he was sorely tempted. He took a deep breath to calm himself, and waited for Rowl to step aside so he and Sam could pass. But Rowl had no intentions of letting them go. He was looking at Sam, an unpleasant smirk on his face. Sam was giving Rowl one of her best don't-you-dare-say-another-word looks. But Rowl thrived on dares, so he had plenty else to say.

"A sweet little maid like you shouldn't be hanging about with a chicken-livered tell-tale like him," Rowl said, swinging the terrible sack until it hit Sam's legs, hard. "He's so feeble, he can't even kill a rat. If a mad dog attacked you, he'd just stand and watch. If someone scoffed at you, he'd just stand and listen. He's not even a real wizard, you know. Not really. He just pretends to be, and spreads tales about how wonderful he is."

"I'll spread you out on the ground if you don't shut up," said Sam.

Rowl laughed. "Try," he said. And before he could blink, Sam bunched her hand into a fist and hit him hard in the stomach.

For a few seconds Rowl didn't move. Slowly, he drew in a long, whistling breath. His face turned red then white, and he gradually doubled over until his head hung between his knees. The bulging sack slipped from his hand, and dark bodies rolled out onto the road. Sam looked away, revolted; then she looked back again, astounded. They were stones! The sack was full of stones!

She shook the stones out, spilling them across the icy dirt, searching eagerly for one that was white. But they were all dark. Disappointed, she looked at Denzil. "We'll never find him," she said.

Denzil stared at her, his mouth hanging open, his eyes full of admiration. "You walloped him," he said.

"Doesn't make any difference," Sam said in a choking voice. "We still can't find Murgatroyd. I bet he's dead, Denzil. I bet he's in someone's sack somewhere. It's silly looking for a white stone anyway. Even if he was one, he could be in the snow somewhere and we wouldn't see him. He could be buried under straw in a stable, or hiding in a crack in a stone wall.

We'll never find him. I know."

Rowl stood up, slowly. His face was its normal colour again, though his breathing was funny. "A white stone?" he asked, curiously. "Are you looking for a white stone?"

"Pure white," said Denzil. "As big as a rat."

Rowl straightened his back, and the gloating look came into his face again. "When all the rats disappeared," he said, "I started finding all these smooth stones. I've been collecting them. They're just right for slinging at the toads, in summer. I've got a white one. It's got little bits of pale pink on it, at both ends."

"Murgatroyd's nose and ears, and his tail," whispered Sam.

"Where is it?" asked Denzil.

Rowl swung the club casually. He gave a malicious little smile. "Don't have to tell you," he said.

"Yes you do," said Denzil. "Is it at your home?"

"Nope," said Rowl. "I'm not saying where it is."

Denzil gripped Rowl's shirt, and pulled downwards until Rowl's shoulders were bowed and Rowl's face was level with his own. "Tell me where it is!" hissed Denzil.

Rowl poked Denzil's ribs with the club, hard, and Denzil yelped. Still, he didn't let Rowl go. Rowl hit him on the legs with the club, and Sam tried to stop him. She grabbed the club, and Rowl kicked her. Denzil clung to Rowl, yelling at him to say where the white stone was; and Rowl started swinging the club wildly, not caring who got hit, or where. The club caught Sam on the side of her head. Half blinded with fury and pain, she flung herself at Rowl and punched him with all her strength.

It was a bitter fight. Though it was two against one, Rowl was winning because he was older and bigger than the other two, and he had the club. At some stage Sam and Denzil became aware of people standing around watching, cheering Rowl on; and then they realised that the cheers came from Rowl's friends, and those friends were beginning to join in.

Sam was flung to the ground, and someone's foot connected hard with the back of her head. Afraid now, she struggled to get up, but there were too many feet and legs about, kicking her. She screamed at Denzil.

A strange darkness came, blocking everything else out. Wind blew, and a great beating sound surrounded her, seemed to be a part of her; then she was free, beyond the fighting and the yelling and the dust.

She opened her eyes and saw the street a long way below, and boys' upturned faces looking at her, open-mouthed with wonder. She turned her head, and saw that she was flying, her wings black and shining in the winter skies; and a hawk flew close beside her.

"Denzil!" she said, but her voice was a strange harsh cry. The hawk flew on ahead, shrieking with joy; and she followed, knowing instinctively how to swoop and turn, and how to soar on the updrafts of the winds.

It was an awesome, joyous time, and Sam would remember it all her life. But at last she and Denzil swooped low over the ground outside Valvasor's door, and she turned and spread her wings wide against the wind, and let its force brake her speed until she dropped, smooth and slow, onto the icy ground. A dark mist enveloped her; there was a rustling of wings, of flight feathers shifting and changing shape, of the brilliant newness of wings giving way to something old and familiar and loved. She looked down, and saw the rough-woven medieval skirt blowing in the wind against her legs. She raised her hands and touched her face, and knew it was her own. She looked beside her, and saw Denzil.

He grinned. "Great, was it not?" he said.

She said nothing, but looked briefly around to make sure no one was watching. Then she slipped her arm around Denzil's neck, and kissed his cheek. "Thank you. It was the best thing that's ever happened to me," she said.

Denzil went very red, and tried hard to wipe the smile off his face.

He couldn't.

"I'm not going back without him," said Sam.

"You have to," said Denzil quietly, cooing to the baby while he squeezed warm milk out of the rag and into its screaming mouth. "I'll finish feeding the waif, then I'll give you the spell. All you've got to do is read it.

I'll hold Valvasor's Time talisman over you, and you'll be home quicker than a blink."

"Not without Murgatroyd."

"But we can't *find* him, can we? We don't even know if the white stone that Rowl has, *is* Murgatroyd. He could have a baby rabbit, for all we know, or a *piglet*. Please, Sam. Go home before Valvasor gets back. I'll look for Murgatroyd every day, and when I find him I'll send him on to you. I promise."

"What happens if someone's killed him?"

"I'll send him back in a special little coffin."

"Denzil!"

"Don't yell. You'll upset the waif."

"I'll upset more than the waif if we don't find Murgatroyd. I'll upset Valvasor when he gets back. I'll see him and tell him everything you've done and ask him to undo it."

"No. Don't tell him. Please, Sam." Denzil's hands shook as he fed the baby, and he started to look desperate. "Look," he said, "we'll do a trade. I'll turn a brown rat into a white one, and train him to do all Murgatroyd's tricks. You'll never tell the dif—"

"Yes, I will. Don't try to wriggle out of it, Denzil. I want — "

She stopped, listening. The drums were beating again, and in the distance people shouted.

"The hunt!" cried Sam. "They've started the hunt again!"

She rushed to the door, and flung it open. Outside,

sparrows were sitting on the snow, ruffling their feathers and looking sleepy and bewildered.

She slammed the door shut behind her and went back to Denzil. He was putting the baby back into Valvasor's bed. Sam noticed that the child was wet and should be changed, but she had more vital things on her mind. "The spell's worn off," she said. "The stones are gone. The people are killing the rats again."

Denzil straightened up and went over to the table. He spread a parchment on the ancient wood and placed a candlestick near it. Sam noticed strange words that rhymed, and which were smudged with interesting blobs of ink.

"You have to help!" she said. "You got me into this. You get me out — with my Mickey Mouse watch that Grandad gave me, and Murgatroyd!"

Denzil said nothing, just stood staring at the spell and biting his lower lip.

"All right then," said Sam, sounding suddenly calm and very purposeful, "I'll do something myself. I'll dress up as an angel again, and command the people to stop killing the rats. They'll listen to an angel."

She went out to the stable and got her wings. When she came inside again, Denzil was writing something else on the spell, changing it. He was looking very worried.

Sam ignored him. She tore off the blue dress, and noticed that some of the pins had come out of the hem of her angel's gown. Taking it off, she pulled them all out and threw them in the fireplace, in case she trod on one. She pulled the white dress back on, then cleaned the wings as best she could and tried to strap them on. Denzil came over to help, and she noticed that he was shaking. She was shaking a bit herself, and beginning to be extremely nervous. The tumult was very close now, and Sam and Denzil could hear people yelling, clubs banging on the ground, and frightened rats squealing.

At last Sam was ready. She looked at Denzil, and saw that his face was white in spite of its dirt. "While I'm talking to them," she said, "you get that spell right, and go and look for Murgatroyd again."

She opened the door, hitched the wings a little higher on her shoulders, took a deep breath, and went out.

Snowy wind rushed over her, and she got goosebumps from cold and terror. The people were crowded together in a bunch, screaming with excitement, and urging one another on. For a few moments they didn't notice the angel, they were so busy with their bloodied clubs and pitchforks. Then the front ones noticed her, and stopped, slowly lowering their weapons. The women stopped banging their drums, and the people at the back, realising that something unexpected was happening, became silent and still. Many people made the sign of the cross on their chests, and knelt on the snowy ground.

Slowly, stumbling a little because her feet were

already frozen numb, Sam went over to them.

"I have a message for you," she said.

The people waited, kneeling, their weapons beside them on the ground, forgotten. Sam licked her lips. Her breath made mists in the air, and she was shivering. Her mind went blank.

"What is the message, Divine One?" asked a man.

"It's a message about the rats," stammered Sam. But her teeth were chattering so much from the cold, the words didn't come out right. She looked at the people kneeling there, trusting her, honouring her, and somehow it seemed all wrong.

But before she could say another word, a man rushed up with a little girl in his arms. Sam noticed that other people scrambled aside, and would not let him near them. The man carried the girl up to Sam. His eyes were full of tears, and his voice was hoarse from grief.

"This is my child, Milda," he said, standing in front of Sam. "I have brought her so that she might be healed. She has the plague."

Sam felt worse than ever. "I can't heal the plague," she said.

Tears rolled down the man's face. "I know," he said, "but the Christ Child can. May I take her to Him?"

"He's . . . He's asleep just now," Sam said.

"May I lay Milda at the door, so that even His presence might work a marvel?"

"If you want to," said Sam. As the man stepped past

her, Sam saw Milda's face. The child was about four, and looked tired and feverish. All over her face were small spots, some red like tiny pimples, some like little yellow blisters, and some were scabs. As Sam watched, a little hand went up and Milda scratched her spots, irritably. The hand, too, was covered in spots.

"Are those itchy?" asked Sam, and the man stopped.

Little Milda's eyes were like saucers, as she looked at the angel's face. "Oh, yeth," Milda lisped. "They're ath itchy ath anything."

"It is a peculiar plague," Milda's father said, "and she is taking a cruelly long time to die."

"I think I'm not dying yet," said Milda, with a bright-eyed smile. "I think I feel better, and my headache'th gone, tho' I'm hot and thirthty all the time."

Sam went closer, and pulled open Milda's blankets. The child was sewn into her clothes, but Sam pushed up the rough woollen sleeves and saw that Milda's arms, too, were covered in spots, some red and angry, some already dried and falling off.

Sam started to smile, and then to laugh. "You haven't got the Black Death!" she said. "You've got chickenpox! I had that, last year. Just exactly the same as you. My spots itched too. But I got better in a few days. So will you."

Milda's father looked at Sam as if she had just performed a miracle. "Then it is not plague?" he asked. "We are all spared?"

"It's chickenpox," said Sam. "Some of you others might get it, but you won't die of it."

"I'm glad," whispered Milda. Then, smiling shyly, she put her hand in a small bag hanging at her waist, and drew out a shining red object.

"My brother found thith," she said. "He sayth it'th magic."

Sam stared at the thing in the child's hand. It was her watch. The red Mickey Mouse watch that her grandfather had given her. Sam was about to explain and ask for it back, when Milda cradled the watch close to her heart, and said: "There'th a little fieldmouse in the magic thing, with a big nothe and a tail and little yellow handth that go round and round. He'th alive. I can hear hith heart beating. He'th making me better." And she smiled again, shyly, beautifully.

"You'd better keep him," said Sam, though the words were hard to say. "Look after him. He's precious."

"I know," said Milda, slipping the watch carefully into the bag again.

An old woman came forward and bowed low. "Could you heal me warts, darlin'?" she asked.

"I'm sorry," Sam said. "I have to go . . ."

But other people were arriving, carrying sick children. A cripple was swinging painfully along on his crutches, and a man was sitting in the snow tearing off his wrinkled hose so he could show the angel the sores on his legs. Several came with toothache, their swollen, aching jaws wrapped in scarves against the cold.

Then Sam noticed Emmeline standing nearby, her hand held by a grey-haired woman, probably her mother. Emmeline's face was uplifted as she listened, and was bright with joy.

"I know your voice, Angel," Emmeline said, very quietly. "You visited me, and touched my eyes . . ."

Just then a huge snowy owl flew low, close to Sam's head, and she felt the wind from the wide beating wings. He carried a white rat in his claws, carefully, and as he flew past, he dropped it straight into Sam's hands.

"Murgatroyd!" she cried, laughing. Murgatroyd climbed up her arm and nestled against her cheek, his whiskers quivering.

The people started talking quietly, and Sam heard the words: " 'Tis a sign from above! A rat as white as snow, and loved by an angel of heaven itself! Surely even these beasts are the Good Lord's, and precious to Him!"

"We'd best not be squashin' them all then!" said someone else. "We'd best be getting along to our homes, and putting out cheese for the poor half-starved little creatures to eat!"

"Aw, that's going a bit far," grumbled someone else. "Bread maybe, but not me wife's good cheese . . ."

Sam didn't say anything; she just smiled and cuddled Murgatroyd.

High in the windy skies a white owl flew, hooting madly. And along the wintry road, looking straight at Sam, came a wizard with a proud and lordly walk, and a face like a stern king.

9 The Christmas Child

ometimes," said Valvasor to Denzil, "I don't know whether you're an exceptionally good wizard who excels at organising things, or whether you're an incurably bad wizard who has incredibly good luck."

"He's an excellent wizard," said Sam, grinning at Denzil over her roast chicken, and then smiling at Valvasor. "But good luck helps."

"It certainly does," said Valvasor, wiping his hands on a white cloth. "And you're going to need lots of it, shortly."

Denzil and Sam both stared at him, their half-chewed chicken bones still in their hands. Denzil stuck out his tongue and slowly licked the gravy that trickled down his chin.

"What do you mean, master?" he asked.

Valvasor's face was very serious. "My son, do you remember the spell you used that brought Sam here?"

Denzil gulped. "Well . . . I don't remember it exactly," he said, "but I don't need it, anyway. I've found another one that'll do."

"Another one won't do," said Valvasor. "It won't do, at all. The same spell that brought Samantha here must be used again, to send her home. Tell me, Denzil, how did that spell work?"

"Um . . . Well, Sam had to say the words too," said Denzil. "I sent them to her, and she had to say them at the same time I said them. It wasn't all that hard. We're good friends, you see."

"Exactly," said Valvasor. "So which good friend is Samantha going to send the spell to, when she wants to go back? She'll need someone who is thinking about her, who believes passionately in magic, and who is good at receiving words across long distances of time and space."

"She's got heaps of friends," said Denzil. "There's her mother and her father and her sister and her brother and all her friends at that awful place she calls school, and she knows hundreds of people in the TV box, and — "

"But they don't all believe in magic," said Sam. "Not really. Since you've been gone, Denzil, Dad laughs about it a bit, and thinks maybe you were just a very good magician. Mum doesn't say much; she doesn't want to argue with Dad, I think. Theresa thinks you were clever, but she doesn't think you used magic. Travis believes a bit in magic, but he keeps quiet about it. There's no one who believes in it as much as I do. I don't know who I could send a spell to."

Denzil looked shaken. "Oh, Gawd," he said.

97

"You're going to have to pray harder than that," said Valvasor.

"But you're cleverer than anyone," said Denzil, looking pleadingly at the great wizard. "You can send Sam home. You can do anything."

"I can do my own great magic," said Valvasor, "and I can undo my magic. But this time the magic does not depend on me, or you. It depends on Samantha herself."

"But I'm not a wizard!" wailed Sam.

"I know," said Valvasor gently. "But you can be trained. You will, however, have to be taught by a woman. That's the way it is, with magic."

"Mother Wyse!" cried Denzil. "She can teach Sam!"

"Mother Wyse?" repeated Sam doubtfully, putting down her chicken.

Valvasor nodded. "There is no need to look alarmed, my dear. Mother Wyse may be a little terrifying to look at, but she is good at heart, and very clever. You will soon learn the magic that is necessary."

"I'm not afraid of her," said Sam. "I think I've already met her, anyway. I think she was the old lady, Mrs Utherwyse, who moved in next door the day you arrived, Denzil. I think she came to our world to keep an eye on you. No one else saw her; only me."

Denzil looked amazed. "She went to your world? So she could look after me?"

Sam nodded. "At least I think it was her," she said. "She looks a bit different, now. More chicken-ish."

"I wish she *was* a chicken," said Denzil furiously, tearing the meat off another bone. "I've got a few things I'd do to her before I shoved her in the cauldron."

Valvasor looked shocked. "That is hardly the way to talk of a friend, Denzil," he said.

"She's not a friend!" snarled Denzil. "She told you all about the magic I made, before. She double-crossed me."

A small smile played about Valvasor's mouth, and one black eyebrow rose. "But I knew all the time, Denzil. No one opens my books without my knowledge, and certainly no one touches my sacred charms without my being immediately aware of it. Mother Wyse didn't tell tales. But we did discuss you and your travels."

"Why didn't you punish me?" asked Denzil. "I broke all your rules."

"But you broke them in order to save me from a terrible fate," said Valvasor. "For that I can only admire your bravery and your loyalty."

Denzil went red. "Thanks," he mumbled.

"The thanks is all mine," smiled Valvasor. "But we don't have much time for talk. Samantha must go to Mother Wyse immediately, and begin her training."

"Will I be home by Christmas?" asked Sam, feeling suddenly nervous, and wishing she could stay here with Denzil.

"You will," said Valvasor. He looked at the angel's

snowy gown and the shining wings, draped over his chair by the fire. "I shall hide your gown and wings until you are ready to return," he said. "It would never do for the village folk to discover that their marvel-worker had wings with wondrously affixing straps, and buttons on her gown. They'd want me to set up a sewing shop with marvellous new fastenings. I don't have an ambition to be a tailor."

Sam smiled, and noticed that her gown and wings had vanished. In a way, she was sorry; she would never get used to her medieval dress with its bumpy seams and itchy weave. And the stockings had fleas in them, she was sure.

Denzil got up and lit several large candles from the fire. It was evening now, and a bitter wind howled outside. The baby woke, and Sam picked it up and cuddled it. Denzil collected up the dishes and washed them in the stream outside. He hadn't been back more than a few minutes when there was a hammering at the door. He went to answer it.

The village folk stood there, shivering in the darkening air. When they saw Denzil, they bowed respectfully. Then one of the men stepped up.

"We would like your permission to visit this house tomorrow," he said. "We would like to bring gifts."

Denzil was puzzled, but the gifts sounded a nice idea. "That's fine," he said. "If you're wondering what to bring, I wouldn't mind some bagpipes. If you can't get— "

"The gifts are for the Christ Child," the man said. "They are in return for His marvels for us."

"Marvels?" gulped Denzil.

The man nodded. "The Child can do great things for us," he said, his voice hushed with reverence and hope. "He can heal all our warts and broken toes and coughs and bruises. Ploughman would like his sick ox to recover, and Mother Gurtler is praying for her stolen chickens to reappear. And Emmeline . . . well, she didn't ask, but we'd all be mighty grateful if the Holy Child would make her see."

"And," said a tiny woman called Mistress Smallbones, glancing lovingly up at the giant of a man beside her, "by tomorrow night I'd like to be as tall as me lovely husband here."

A fat bald man stepped forward, grinning, and held up a shining comb carved of bone. "The miracle I'd like," he said, "is for the Christ Child to grow back all my hair. I bought this here new comb all ready to do my locks, my faith is so strong."

"We all have great faith," said the first man. "We do not know why God has chosen us, but we are grateful. We will leave the Child to sleep tonight, and in the morning we will come and pay Him homage and give Him our gifts, and wait for our marvels."

Denzil nodded and shut the door. He felt sick, and very worried.

Valvasor and Sam had heard every word. Sam looked amused, but Valvasor's face was grave.

"You have started a grand thing, Denzil," he said. "How do you propose to finish it?"

"I think I'll go for a holiday," said Denzil.

"I think not," said Valvasor.

Denzil chewed his lower lip. "I could tell them the truth, I suppose," he said.

"That is one solution," said Valvasor.

"I think *you* should tell them," said Denzil.

For a while Valvasor was silent. "Sometimes, Denzil," he said, very quietly, "it is best not to destroy people's dreams."

"You mean, they can still come tomorrow, for all their marvels?" cried Denzil, astounded. "But who'll do them?"

Valvasor said nothing, but his eyes pierced deep into Denzil's soul.

"Me?" cried Denzil. "Do I have to do it all?"

"Either you," said Valvasor, "or that obstreperous offspring in Samantha's arms."

Denzil groaned and covered his face with his hands. "I can't!" he wailed, louder than the baby. "Oh, Mother Mary, Saint Theresa, anyone else who's listening — tell me what to do!"

"I have a suggestion," said Valvasor. Denzil looked up, his face bright with hope. "You could dust my books," said the ancient wizard, with a shrewd smile. "They might accidentally fall open at the right place, and — with a stroke of incredibly good luck — you just might happen to mutter the right words. It's worth a try. Wizards have found lost chickens before, and warts have a way of magically disappearing."

Denzil shot Sam a cheerful grin, and went to find the feather duster.

Thinking she had an evening of spells and wild wizardry ahead, Sam settled into Valvasor's big chair and rocked the baby. But she was startled, and half afraid, when Valvasor took the child and tucked it into his bed, then handed Sam a thick green woollen cloak and a pair of Denzil's high winter boots.

"While my apprentice is sorting out the marvels," Valvasor said to Sam, "I'll take you to Mother Wyse."

It was a wild night. Snow whirled all around, and strange animals wailed and howled in the fields around the tiny village. Mother Wyse lived along Summer Lane, which was a pleasant path in summer but was a muddy trough of garbage and melted snow in the winter.

Sam slipped and slithered in the slush, and she could feel Murgatroyd scrambling around in the little cane cage Valvasor had given her for him. She could hardly see the wizard as he strode ahead, his black cloak swirling about him. After a while Valvasor took Sam's hand and walked with her. She felt safer then, though she noticed that his hand was very warm, and strange vibrations came from him. She supposed it was his power, since he was a great wizard.

They came, at last, to a solitary cottage surrounded

by dark and windswept fields. To Sam it looked different from the cottage she'd seen dropped onto Valvasor's floor; but then she'd seen it from her perch above, in the loft, and now she saw it from the muddy ground outside. There were no windows in the cottage, but some of the ancient stones had fallen out and red light glimmered through the cracks and spaces in the walls. Valvasor banged on the door and it was thrown open.

"Come in, Valvasor!" cackled an old voice, and they went in. The door banged shut behind them.

By a firepit sat Mother Wyse, spinning. Her hair was more tangled than ever. She was wearing loose black robes with posies of herbs pinned onto them. Her hands, Sam noticed, were amazingly wrinkled, her fingers bent like crooked claws, yet they spun smoothly and skilfully, and never faltered or trembled. The firelight flickered over the woman's face, and her eyes, sharp and birdlike, burned with golden lights. A black cat lay curled on her lap, dark as midnight against the white apron.

"Hello, dearie," croaked the old woman, smiling cheerfully at Sam. "Come and sit by the fire and warm yourself. And you too, old friend."

"I cannot stay," said Valvasor loudly. "This is Samantha. Denzil brought her here on a Connecting-Word. Now she needs the power to send the Word herself, to someone at her home. Will you teach her, please?"

"Aye, that I will," said Mother Wyse, never halting in her spinning. "I'll teach her well, and send her back to you in two days."

"You have my gratitude," said Valvasor, turning to leave. Over his shoulder he said: "And my apprentice's gratitude, I don't doubt."

Then he was gone.

10 *Magic Going Right*

ell, don't stand there staring, Agapantha," said Mother Wyse. "If you want to make a suspecting-bird, you've got to think about it. They don't just come when you snap your fingers, you know. And if you want to send it to Rome, you'd better do it before Christmas, or it won't get there until next year. You want to send it for a Christmas gift, I suppose?"

Wondering what a suspecting-bird was, Sam sat down on the spare stool beside the old woman. "Actually, I have to make a Connecting-Word," said Sam, staring at Mother Wyse's face, and not really certain whether the old woman had been Mrs Utherwise.

"A Connecting-Word?" cried Mother Wyse, stopping spinning for a moment or two. "Whatever for? Has Weasel gone and got himself misplaced again? He really should stop meddling in magic until he's a bit wiser. I tried to tell him that but he won't listen. He's a bit too hot-headed for his own good, that one."

"Denzil's fine," said Sam. "I'm the one who has to

get home. I have to go to Londfield, seven hundred years ahead."

"Seven hundred deer, dead?" asked Mother Wyse, shocked. "Oh dear, they'll make a frightful smell."

"*Seven hundred years ahead!*" shouted Sam, and the black cat opened one glowing eye and glared at her. "I have to go home to Londfield, seven hundred years into the future."

"You'll need a Connecting-Word, child," said Mother Wyse.

Sam sighed. "I know," she said.

Mother Wyse put the cat down on the hearth and went over to her book shelves. They were crammed with books; beautiful, thick old books with golden lettering on the spines. The old woman took one down. She blew on it, sending a cloud of dust shimmering in the firelight. She came back to Sam, and gave her the book.

"Find a picture you like, dearie," she said, then went over to a huge chest and took out a rolled mattress. The mattress was thin, and straw poked out of holes in it. She put it on the floor by the fire and went back to the chest for blankets and furs.

For a long time Sam looked at the book. It was made by hand, the paper thick and rough like paper Sam had made once at school. The book was full of pictures, all of them beautifully painted, and marvellous. There were castles with flags that really flew; knights fighting, whose armour shone and flashed, and whose swords rang loudly on the shields of their enemies; there were medieval ladies dancing, their long robes swinging as they moved; minstrels whose singing Sam could hear; falcons that flew across painted skies; dragons that really breathed fire and smoke; kings at war, their great armies clashing and thundering; and jesters and acrobats who did wonderful cartwheels right across the page.

At last Sam chose a picture of a king. He was seated on a golden throne, and his crown was only a thin band of gold about his head. But he had a powerful face, and he reminded Sam a lot of Valvasor.

Sam glanced at Mother Wyse, now in the kitchen corner of her house, sprinkling dried leaves into two little bowls.

"I've chosen a picture, Mother Wyse," Sam said.

"Don't tell me what it is, child," said Mother Wyse. "Close the book, and don't say another word. But think about that picture. Look at it again and again, but don't let me see it. Know it through and through, every bit of it."

Then Mother Wyse came and leaned over the fire, and with a large spoon scooped water out of a cauldron hanging above the flames. She poured the steaming water into one of the little bowls, and offered it to Sam. Sam put the book on the dirt floor beside her, took the bowl and sniffed it. She pulled a face.

"What's this?" she asked.

"Camomile tea, dearie. It will help you to sleep

tonight. Drink it up, and then you can go to bed."

But the tea didn't help Sam sleep. She lay awake a long time, worrying. She could see Mother Wyse in the straw bed across the room, with furs and blankets and her black cat piled on top of her. The old woman snored magnificently. A black crow sat on the bedpost, so still that at first Sam thought it was stuffed. But it flapped its wings when the cat hissed at it, and Sam remembered seeing it before — in a red cage and in another time.

Sam watched the firelight dancing over the walls, and tried not to look at the stuffed animals with their bright beady eyes, the gleaming skulls, and the cages of small, living animals. A little monkey sat clutching the bars of his cage, looking at her sadly from across the fire. Quietly, Sam got out of bed and took him out of the cage. He clung to her, his tiny fingers catching in the loose weave of her dress. She snuggled back into the thick, soft furs of her bed, hearing the straw rustling under her. The monkey curled up on the fur near her head, and dozed. In his cage near her head, Murgatroyd sat up like a miniature kangaroo and washed his ears and whiskers.

At last Sam fell asleep, her fingers in the soft fur of the little monkey. She dreamed of a king on a golden throne, and of going home.

Mother Wyse took a handful of dried flies out of a box and gave several to the toads in their cages. She fed all her other animals, made sure they all had clean water, and swept out their cages.

"What do you keep them for?" asked Sam.

"Look at your book, dearie. You'll never learn a Connecting-Word if you sit gazing around all the time. Concentrate. Fixate. Focus."

Sam sighed and looked at the picture of the king. But she was finding it hard to concentrate. It was almost as dark in the cottage during the day as it was at night, and Sam's eyes stung from staring through the smoke. Her throat was sore, and she longed to give her nose a good blow. But she didn't have a tissue, and didn't really want to use her sleeve — not when it wouldn't be washed for a year or so.

She was cold, even though she sat near the fire with a thick fur wrapped around her. From outside came the sound of the bitter wind blowing, and trees cracking beneath their burden of snow. Every now and again the gale whistled through the holes in the ancient stone walls of Mother Wyse's cottage, billowing the skins covering the walls, and puffing smoke into Sam's eyes. The thatched roof creaked and shivered and, sometimes, in a particularly severe gust, Sam thought the whole roof would be blown off. The monkey sat on the warm hearthstones at Sam's feet. Murgatroyd, let out of his cage for an early morning prowl, was inspecting the breakfast bowls still on the bench. From the way he licked ecstatically at the remains of porridge in the bowls, he enjoyed medieval food more than Sam did. He was watched disdainfully by the black cat, who had a taste for hares and hawks but thought rats and mice — especially white ones — were trivial and tasteless.

Sam leaned over the picture of the king, staring hard at his gilt-edged robes of deep purple, the jewelled hilt of his sword, and the golden throne. Behind the throne hung a magnificent tapestry depicting the king's courtiers hunting a stag. They carried bows and arrows, and the stag was bounding away into the forest. The trees were moving in the wind and, while Sam watched, one of the courtiers drew his bow and shot an arrow at the deer. But the arrow fell far short of its target, and Sam was glad of that. Today the king looked a bit like her father. The painted hair was black today, though Sam was sure that yesterday it had been brown.

"Put the book away, Agapantha," said Mother Wyse, coming and sitting down. Sam closed the book, and held her hands towards the fire to warm them.

"Now, dearie," said Mother Wyse, settling herself on a low wooden stool next to Sam, and smiling cheerfully. "This is how you send a Connecting-Word. You think about that picture you have just been looking at."

"Then?" said Sam.

"Then you pass it to me."

"You mean, I cut it out and give it to you?"

"Oh, there's no need to cut anything, dearie," said

Mother Wyse, alarmed. "We're connecting, not dissecting. You give it to me by thought."

"It would be easier to call you on the phone," said Sam, not at all sure about this thought-connecting business.

"Install me on a throne?" chuckled Mother Wyse, delighted, rocking back and forth and almost falling off her stool. "Oh no, dearie! I know I look wonderful, but I don't really go in for all that splendid stuff!"

"I said, *call you on the phone!*" said Sam, giggling.

"Phone?" said Mother Wyse, wiping her streaming eyes on her apron, and screwing up her face while she tried to remember. "Phone? Oh, yes. But there's no need to get scientific. We don't need all those wires and buttons and things. Just our own thoughts. The human mind's a wonderful thing, dearie. A wonderful thing."

"It *was* you in that house next door!" said Sam, smiling. "You came to live next door to me, to keep an eye on Denzil."

"If you'd keep your eyes on that picture," said Mother Wyse, "we might get this Connecting-Word going. Now think, Agapantha. Think hard. Send me that picture you've got in your head."

Sam shut her eyes, screwed up her face with the effort, and imagined the king.

For a long time she held the image of him in her mind, and she was concentrating so hard that she didn't hear Mother Wyse clucking and mumbling beside her. Suddenly the old woman said: "Animal. It's an animal."

Sam opened her eyes. "No," she said.

"Shut them!" cried Mother Wyse. "Hold the picture! Hold it! Now . . . let's see . . ."

Another long silence, while the wind howled and the roof shook.

"It *is* an animal, you know," said Mother Wyse. She cackled, thrilled. "You're a bit sly, aren't you, Agapantha? Trying to trick me? Ha! Didn't work! It's an animal! There's something on its head."

"Gold?" said Sam.

"Mould? Heavens, no! Horn. It's a unicorn. They're hunting it. It's extinct now, you know. The unicorn. They hunted them all to death for their horns. Got magic powers, those horns. Now. Where were we?"

"Up the wrong tree," said Sam. "It's not an animal, Mother Wyse."

"Just keep quiet, dearie, and hold that picture in your head."

Sam sighed, and did as she was told.

"You shouldn't have mentioned trees," said Mother Wyse, after a while. "You shouldn't give me clues. It's a tree. Several trees, in fact. A forest."

"No," said Sam. She hesitated, then added: "I'm sorry, Mother Wyse, but this isn't working. It's not an animal, or a tree. It's — "

"Hush!" screeched Mother Wyse, jumping up and starting to pace the dirt floor. She walked fast, around

113

and around in circles, her body bent over, tense, her hands clasped behind her. She muttered while she walked, her wild grey hair mingling with the thick smoke in the firelight.

"Bows," she muttered, then paced some more. "Bows. Hunters' bows. I'm sure they're hunting a unicorn."

"There isn't a unicorn," sighed Sam, and tried harder to imagine the king. But all she could think of was her father, and of the time he had dressed up as a medieval jester, and put on a magic show for Denzil. It had been a great day, that . . .

"A man," said Mother Wyse, still pacing, her eyes squinting through the smoke as if seeing distant things. "I see a man."

Sam jumped up, excited, but Mother Wyse yelled and waved at her to sit down. "Don't tell me! Let me find it for myself! A man. A man is what I see, a tall dark man with something on his head."

Sam was very still, her eyes shut tight, and with all her strength she imagined the king with the golden crown.

"A funny hat!" cried Mother Wyse, triumphantly. "He's wearing a funny hat! He's a jester!"

Sam groaned, and Mother Wyse started pacing again, her old wrinkled fists pressed hard to her forehead. "Valvasor," she said. "I see a picture of Valvasor."

"No," said Sam.

"But it's a man," said Mother Wyse.

"Yes."

"A handsome man."

"Yes."

"He's wearing gold."

"Right!" yelled Sam.

"He's got gold on his clothes. Medals! He's a famous soldier!"

"Wrong!" yelled Sam.

"Gold embroidery, then. He's rich!"

"Right!"

"He's a wealthy knight!"

"Wrong!"

"Think, Agapantha! Hold the image!"

"I am!"

Mother Wyse paced faster. "Purple!" she cried. "I see purple!"

"Right!"

"Purple, and a king on golden throne, and a picture of his courtiers hunting a stag!"

"You did it!" screamed Sam, jumping up and flinging her arms around Mother Wyse. The old woman staggered backwards, bowled over by exhaustion and Sam's joy. Fortunately her bed was just behind her, and Mother Wyse collapsed onto it, trembling all over, her eyes brilliant and victorious behind her frenzied hair.

"Well, dearie," she said, sitting up when she had got her breath, and straightening her crumpled clothes, "that's the easy bit done."

"*Easy* bit?" cried Sam. "That was *easy*?"

"Of course," said Mother Wyse, getting up and starting to make some tea. "Pictures are always easy. There are colours, shapes, all sorts of clues. Pictures are simple stuff. Basic. Done in seconds. Now, Agapantha, we make the real magic, the stuff with the real power. Now, we send a *Word*."

11 Magic Going Wrong

enzil chewed on a thick slice of bread and a slab of pale goats' cheese, and dropped crumbs all over Valvasor's priceless book. He brushed the crumbs off, and sighed. He wished Valvasor had stayed to help with the marvels; it wasn't easy conjuring up lost chickens. New chickens — any new bird, for that matter — would have been easy. But Mother Gurtler was very particular about her chickens. There were ten of them, and they all had names. She'd expect the same birds back, with all their special habits and quirks. There'd be no fooling her. She knew which ones had knobs on their legs, which ones had bald patches, and which ones had rips in their combs. And talking of bald patches and combs . . .

Baldie Mason wouldn't be satisfied, either, unless Denzil gave him hair exactly the same as he had before. Baldie often talked of the good old days, when he was a handsome youth with hair so magnificent that all the girls craved to run their fingers through it, and he'd had to fight them off in their hundreds. And now he wanted the same crowning glory back again. He'd forgotten, though, that now he had no teeth, and his handsome face had shrivelled to something like a wrinkled prune. He'd wonder why, when he had all his magnificent hair back, the girls weren't still mobbing him. He'd say Denzil had failed.

"And what about Mistress Smallbones?" wailed Denzil to himself, sinking lower and lower into despair. "She wants to be as tall as that gigantic husband of hers! I'll have to stretch her neck longer than my arm!"

The difficulties almost overwhelmed him. The biggest difficulty of all was Emmeline. There was no magic in the world that would make a blind person see. Emmeline would have to do without her miracle.

Denzil sighed heavily, choked on a crumb, and pored over the book again.

After a while he got the pen and some parchments, and started copying out spells. He had to alter some of them to suit his needs. There was a spell to bring back lost pigeons, and Denzil decided that would have to do. When he had some pigeons, he could turn them into hens. Maybe he could then make a forgetting spell for Mother Gurtler, so she wouldn't notice that her chickens weren't the same as they were before.

The spell to make hair grow was a bit vague, and Denzil wasn't absolutely sure whether it referred to bald humans, or fur rugs that had worn a bit thin.

He'd give it a go, anyway — the worst that could happen was that he'd have to give all Valvasor's fur rugs a haircut. As for Mistress Smallbones, she'd have to be satisfied with however high she ended up, because there was a warning with that spell saying it could not be reversed. Denzil was a bit worried about that, so he wrote out only half the words, just to be safe.

The spell to cure a sick ox was not so simple, because Denzil didn't know exactly what was wrong with the poor beast. But, having been fixed in stone for an hour or two and then turned back into an ox again, it had to be a bit more lively than it was before.

Encouraged, Denzil finished writing out the spells, and read them over one last time to check them. When speaking aloud the magic words it was vital not to hesitate or falter. The slightest mistake could alter the spell and cause unimaginable consequences. A big interruption, especially in this long and complex spell, could bring about untold disaster. So Denzil was very careful that the spell was right; that all he had to do was read it through aloud very, very carefully.

He stood in the middle of the floor, the paper held before him, and began:

"Put a little pigeon
Out of human sight,
Alter it a smidgen,
Turn it snowy white;
Multiply it — "

Behind Denzil, the door opened and closed again, very quietly. He thought it must be Valvasor come home to see how the marvels were going. Denzil didn't bother to turn around. He faltered only a split second, then read on, in a lofty voice:

"Multiply it tenfold
For Mother Gurtler's share,
Chickens in her household —"

Denzil was aware of someone standing close behind him, and of a face peering over his shoulder. It wasn't Valvasor's. He froze, horrified, and three seconds passed. He read on, trying to keep his voice calm and commanding.

"Chickens in her household,
Chickens everywhere —"

"I'm not that thrilled about chickens," said a voice. It was Rowl's. "But I did like the way you turned into a hawk, you and your fair maid, and flew off. That was terrific."

Denzil fought to ignore him. He moved away, so Rowl couldn't read over his shoulder, and carried on. But he'd lost his place, and missed a bit.

". . Restore the ailing oxen,
With the strength of twenty men,
Renew old Baldie's lost locks,
And make them long again.
Make them —"

"Will you stop reading for a while?" said Rowl, going to stand in front of Denzil, and tugging at the bottom of the parchment. "I've come to say I'm sorry. I had no idea you were a real wizard."

"Be *quiet!*" hissed Denzil, and went on quickly:

"Make them long and shining,
Just as they were before,
And let the girls, all sighing,
Come crowding at his door.
And while the power for growing
Is blowing in this place,
Stretch up Mistress Smallbones,
To see her husband's face;
To see him eye to eyeball,
To be as tall as he —"

"I'm sorry I'm interrupting you," said Rowl, a little uneasily, because he could see that Denzil was getting really stressed about something, "but I hoped that we could be friends."

Denzil swore under his breath, lost his place again, and carried on.

". . . umm . . . And all the warts and bruises,
And all the broken bones,
Every sore that oozes,
And —"

"Denzil? Will you please talk to me? I know I must have upset you a lot, but I really do want to be friends. I think you must be the cleverest person in the whole village. Even cleverer than Valvasor. I mean, I know he's a great wizard, but you — you can fly. That's really something, Denzil. That's a marvel."

"Good," said Denzil, through clenched teeth, giving up and tearing the spell to pieces. "I'm glad you think I'm good at marvels. Because nobody else will. You've just made me mess up the biggest spell I've ever worked in this village. Every person I've just tried to help is going to come here in a minute, with a pitchfork to kill me. That's so long as Mistress Smallbones can bend down low enough to see me, and Baldie can chase me without tripping over his miles of hair, and Mother Gurtler can find me through all the hens I've just given her. With another little marvel, I just might be able to escape."

Rowl looked mystified, and hurt. "I don't know anything about hens and hair and stuff," he said. "I came to ask if you'd turn me into a hawk, too, and let me fly with you for a little while."

"All right," said Denzil, furiously hitching up his hose, and pulling so hard that his foot went right through the end. "Where do you want to go, Rowl? France? Scotland? The further away from here, the better. We could even go to the Holy Land — to Bethlehem — though the Christ Child isn't there this Christmas. Oh, Gawd. I forgot about him."

He rushed over to Valvasor's bed and bent over to check the child. It was sleeping peacefully, even snoring a little.

Denzil sat on the bed, and stroked the waif's soft black hair. "I'm sorry I messed up your marvels," he whispered. "But I did try. Honest, I tried."

Rowl shuffled uncomfortably, not understanding at all what was going on. After a few moments, he left, closing the door quietly behind him.

A wondrous sight met his eyes. He stared for a moment, his mouth hanging open. Then he flung open the door again, and yelled at Denzil to come and look.

Sam waved goodbye to Mother Wyse and set off along the muddy lane back to the village. It was a clear day, though it was cold, and she enjoyed the walk. She swung Murgatroyd's cage as she walked, talking to him, and wondering if she could send him a Connecting-Word if he was ever lost again, to bring him back.

As she neared the village, she heard the strangest noise. It was people singing and cheering, children laughing, drums banging and pipes playing, dogs barking, and . . .

Chickens.

There were chickens all over the place! Chickens on the tops of thatched roofs, perched along fences, flapping in the pigpens, teetering on windowsills and doorsteps, and fluttering all along the road.

In the village, it seemed that everyone was in a parade. Wrapped in their bright shawls and cloaks, and with their winter mittens and scarves and long pointed hats, the people looked like something out of an old-fashioned movie. They danced and sang in the snow, laughing and cheering. Mistress Smallbones was prancing about with her head held high on her long, elegant neck. She had her right arm through her husband's; and he, big though he was, looked up at her with pride and adoration in his eyes. She did look grand.

Baldie — and Sam hardly recognised him — was doing a slow, majestic dance, flinging back his long mane of red-gold hair, and bowing to all the girls who giggled and admired him. Master Ploughman, prouder than he'd ever been, was coming along the road with his huge old ox. The animal was as lively as a young calf, and its coat shone black as coal against the snow.

Mother Gurtler was doing a jig with five chickens in her arms, singing their names, and glancing lovingly around at the hundred or so other hens that followed her. Sam walked on, smiling to herself, marvelling at Denzil's talent. But she was a bit worried that someone might recognise her as the angel, so she tucked her bright curls under her hood, bent her head low, and walked quickly along the edge of the crowd towards Valvasor's door.

She was almost there when she noticed a motionless figure a little way apart from the others, standing tall and tranquil, and looking towards Valvasor's house. It was Emmeline. Sam was about to go over to her, but a little girl ran up to Emmeline to show her something. The girl was Little Milda, recovered from her chickenpox now, and she held a small red object.

Watching them, Sam noticed that Emmeline laughed and lifted her hand straight away to touch the watch, as if she saw it. Sam wished she could go and talk to them, but she dared not. Little Milda would be bound to recognise Sam as the angel, and the whole terrible hoax would be revealed.

Sam stumbled the last few steps through a fluster of frantic hens, and reached Valvasor's door. Denzil stood there, grinning like an imp. Rowl was with him.

"Sam!" cried Denzil, beaming, then immediately trying to look cool. "How was your visit with Mother Wyse?"

"It was terrific," said Sam.

"You visited old Battybird?" asked Rowl, astounded.

"I stayed with her," said Sam.

Rowl's surprise turned to admiration, and he grinned. "By all the saints, you're braver than I am!" he said. Then he turned to Denzil. "I'll go now. Can we go flying tomorrow?"

To Sam's amazement, Denzil nodded. As Rowl went away, a loud, furious wailing came from inside the house.

Denzil groaned. "Feeding time again," he said. "He'll be wet, too, for sure. I'll heat up some milk, and you can look after the messy end."

"You're a real hero," said Sam, and they went inside.

12 The Return Home

alvasor wrapped the waif warmly in a fur, and settled it snugly in a sling under his cloak.

"I'll be gone four days," he said. "I am taking the waif to a town about two days' flight from here. It will be well loved. I've told the village folk here that the Christ Child is going back to Bethlehem, where he belongs. They are grateful for the short time that he was here. They will talk about these marvels for many years, Denzil. And they will talk about the angel."

The great wizard smiled at Sam. She was dressed in her angel clothes again, and her wings, newly-cleaned by magic, shone brightly behind her golden hair.

"For a hundred years, this time will be remembered," went on Valvasor. "Parents will tell their children, and their children will tell their children. Your brightness will not be forgotten, Samantha."

"I wish they would forget me," said Sam, in a low

voice. "I don't feel right, pretending to be an angel. I feel as if I've told a huge lie."

"You have told no lies," said Valvasor, "and you did not come here to deceive people."

"But I have deceived them," said Sam, "because what they believe isn't true."

"Is happiness a true and real thing?" asked Valvasor.

"Yes," said Sam.

"Is kindness true, when we give things to people that make them glad?"

Sam nodded.

"And love," said Valvasor. "Is love true?"

"Yes," said Sam.

"Then I would say that the angel they believe in is true," said Valvasor. "Now, are you sure you can work the Connecting-Word?"

"Positive," said Sam, smiling.

"Then I will bid you farewell, child," said Valvasor. "Perhaps one day we shall meet again."

"I hope so," said Sam. "If it gets boring at home, I'll dress up as something different, and come back."

"Mother Wyse was supposed to tell you how to *leave!*" cried Denzil, alarmed. "She wasn't supposed to tell you how to *come back!*"

"What Mother Wyse taught Sam is between themselves," said Valvasor, "and is none of our business."

He gave Sam a wink. "Work your magic, child," he

said. "I'll stay to see you return to your own place, then I too will be gone."

Denzil put a little stool in the middle of the floor. Just in front of it he put the gold and silver Time talisman.

Sam sat down, holding on her knee the little cage with Murgatroyd in it. She still longed for her Mickey Mouse watch, but knew it would be well looked after. And she had instead a little carved fox, which she would love for as long as she lived.

She gave Denzil a small smile. "I hate goodbyes," she said.

"So do I," he said, "so hurry it up."

"It's your turn to visit me, next time," she reminded him. Then she closed her eyes and thought of her brother, Travis.

* * *

Travis glanced at his mother. She was sitting on the sofa in the lounge, looking pale but peaceful. Mr MacAllister was sitting beside her, giving her a cup of tea.

"It'll help you calm down, darling," Mr MacAllister said. "When you're feeling better, we'll go and report this to the police."

"I'm feeling fine," said Mrs MacAllister quietly. "There's no need to call the police. Sam's only been gone five minutes. I've just had a bit of a shock, that's all."

"Mum's right," said Travis from the doorway. "There's no point in calling the police. Sam wasn't kidnapped, Dad. She's with Denzil."

"Don't be ridiculous," said Mr MacAllister. "Sam's been kidnapped. You didn't see anything, Travis — you had your head stuck in that oil-dripping doohickey you call a car. Whatever happened to Sam gave your mother such a shock, she fainted. This is serious, Travis."

"I'm not saying it isn't," said Travis, "but what I am saying is that it's no use calling the police. What are they going to do? Zoom off with their lights flashing and sirens screaming, and break the time barrier through to someone's barnyard, run over all their chickens, blow the thatch off a few cottages, and scare the living daylights out of people who have never seen anything faster than a windmill? Get real, Dad! The police can't possibly find Sam. She disappeared the same way Denzil did, when he went home. She's with him. I'll bet my car on it."

"I wouldn't want that old heap," said Mr MacAllister. "And don't you tell me to get real. I'm the only one around here talking any sense! Whatever optical illusions Denzil used to make himself disappear, he couldn't possibly travel through time. It was all a hoax — carefully planned and brilliantly pulled off — but a hoax just the same. Denzil was a clever magician, that's all. He might have fooled you all with that medieval stuff, but he didn't fool me! No, Sam's been kidnapped, and the sooner the police are onto it, the better."

"I hope she remembers to keep herself clean," murmured Mrs MacAllister anxiously.

"Clean?" said Mr MacAllister. "What's keeping clean got to do with being kidnapped?"

"Well, Denzil hardly ever bathed, at home," Mrs MacAllister said. "Those people were awfully dirty, back in those times. I'd hate her to get an infection, or fall sick or something. I hope she's safe. I hope she sticks with Denzil, and doesn't eat anything that hasn't been cooked properly, and stays away from people with diseases. She'll have to have a good bath when she gets back. And you'll have to fumigate her clothes, dear, and her angel's wings."

"For goodness' sake!" spluttered Mr MacAllister. "She's been abducted in someone's car — she's not touring around some prehistoric village infested with the Black Death!"

"Denzil's village isn't prehistoric," said his wife, quietly sipping her tea. "His times are very well documented in history books and encyclopaedias. And Denzil wouldn't let anything awful happen to her, I'm sure. He's a caring, sensible boy."

Mr MacAllister made a snorting noise that was meant to be a laugh.

Travis left them and went back to his car. He didn't feel like changing the oil filter now, so he cleaned his hands on a rag and sat on the back step of the porch, to think.

"I wonder where you are, Sam," he said. He buried his head in his hands and tried to imagine the place where she might be. He thought of castles, hilltops with dragons' caves, and great halls with kings feasting in them. None of it seemed right, somehow.

Then he imagined a thatched roof, and walls of stone. There was snow all around, and hundreds of chickens. The chickens seemed a bit odd, but the rest of it felt right. Then he saw inside the house; saw a fur rug, and skins on an ancient wooden floor. He saw the beautiful gold and silver medallion that Denzil had worn; and behind it, wearing funny little handmade shoes with pointed toes, two feet. His eyes moved upwards. He saw a snow-white skirt, and the lower part of a girl sitting down. There was a small cane cage on her lap. He saw Murgatroyd in the cage, and almost laughed aloud. He looked up further; saw the shape of wings, and golden hair, and the face of a girl sitting with her eyes screwed shut, as if she were thinking hard.

"Sam!" he shouted.

For an instant Sam's eyes opened. She sat upright and very still, as if she listened. Then she closed her eyes again. The scene faded. No matter how hard he tried, Travis could not imagine it again. But odd words came to him, meaningless and disconnected.

He shook his head, got up, and went inside for a beer.

He took a can out of the fridge and went outside again. He felt unsettled and on edge, as if someone were calling him but he couldn't quite make out what they said.

He sat down on the step again, and was about to pull the tab off the top of the can when he noticed something odd. The name on the beer can was wrong. All the words were wrong. He stared at them, puzzled and astounded.

In awesome flight
Through time and space . . .

Frowning, Travis turned the can over and over in his hands. The letters were jumbling, tumbling over and over one another like pieces of paper in the wind. He thought of Sam again, and the words settled into order. He smiled to himself, knowing that something powerful and extraordinary was happening.

"Go on, Sam," he said. "I'm receiving you, loud and clear."

* * *

Denzil bent down and stared hard into Sam's face.

"It's not working," he said.

"It is," said Sam. "Be quiet."

"No it's not. You're still here."

"Be quiet, lad," said Valvasor, very softly. "We must not interrupt a Word. And stand aside, or you might be caught away with her."

Denzil scuttled backwards, and held on tightly to the heavy planks of the table. Sam's eyes were still closed. "Beer," she said. "He's drinking a can of beer."

Valvasor looked bewildered. "Ale," whispered Denzil, knowledgeably. "They brew it in shiny little barrels, which they rip open and drink all in one go."

"Good Lord," murmured Valvasor, shocked. "They must get mightily inebriated. He'll never receive her Word, if he's befuddled by ale."

"He'll be all right," said Denzil. "He's never befuddled. He's brave and strong. He's a black knight with a shining helmet and a motorbike."

"No he's not," said Sam. "He's got a car, now . . ."

But her voice was very faint. When Denzil and Valvasor looked towards the place where she had sat, the stool was empty.

Sam had gone home.

13 The True Marvel

enzil tramped slowly along the muddy track to Mother Wyse's cottage. It was Christmas Day, and he carried a small bag containing gifts for her, from himself and Valvasor. The great wizard was still away taking the waif to a far town, and Denzil was looking forward to Mother Wyse's company. It had been lonely in the village, as everyone had gone to the neighbouring town for the festivities there. They'd all be dancing and singing and playing music, and jugglers would be there, and fiddlers, and people playing trumpets. They'd be having a grand time. Still, thought Denzil, trudging along in the slush, Valvasor will be home tonight, and we'll have our Christmas goose with Mother Wyse, and go to the town tomorrow . . .

Just then, he noticed someone in the field beside the road. It was a girl in a grey dress and a blue hood and cloak. She was playing with a pack of young foxes, feeding them scraps of bread, and flinging them sticks to chase. Denzil watched for a while, but then one of the foxes saw him, and they all fled, yelping, rust-red against the snow. The girl looked up.

It was Emmeline.

"It's me — Denzil!" he called out.

Emmeline came towards him, her footprints deep blue across the white. To Denzil's amazement, she came directly to him, and when she stood on the track he saw that she was looking at his face, and that her eyes were dark like sapphires and as shining as the sky.

"Christmas blessings, Denzil," she said, smiling. "You're smaller than I imagined you. In the village they say that you are a wizard of great excellence, and that your power is a fearful thing. But I saw the snowman you made with the children yesterday, and though it looks uncannily real, it is comical and festive, and has a merry face."

Denzil couldn't speak for a while. Then, his voice husky and incredulous, he said: "You can see, Emmeline."

"Aye, I can," she replied. "Your angel visited me, that day the people were all out killing rats. She came and touched my eyes. And now I see."

"Blimey," said Denzil, in a choking voice.

They parted, and he ran all the way to Mother Wyse's house. He burst inside, not bothering to knock, and found her bending over her cauldron, tasting something steaming from a spoon.

"Saints alive, Weasel!" she spluttered, dropping the

spoon in the cauldron. "Why don't you drop in with a blaze of light, and frighten me properly?"

"Sorry," he murmured. "I've just seen Emmeline. She's healed, Mother Wyse! She can see!"

"'Tis not so surprising," murmured Mother Wyse, pushing her hair out of her eyes, and fishing with a stalk of rhubarb for the lost spoon. "With all your wizardry, and an angel visitor, and the Christ Child being found in Valvasor's stable, I'm not at all surprised that there have been one or two marvels."

"But she wasn't a real angel!" cried Denzil.

"Not an ideal angel? I'd have thought she was perfect! What do you expect an ideal angel to do — flutter around in that wonderful galaxy you saw once, and fight with swords of light? It's a beautiful thing, for an angel to make a blind person see. I wouldn't complain about it, Weasel. You and I couldn't do that, not with the best magic in the world."

She found the spoon, and placed it on the floor by the firepit. Then she sat on a stool, and pointed to one for Denzil.

"I'm not complaining," Denzil said, sitting down. "I just don't understand it. Sam wasn't a real angel. She was a girl. Just an ordinary girl."

"Who's Sam?" said Mother Wyse.

"You know. You taught her how to make the Connecting-Word."

"Agapantha? Agapantha was the angel?"

"Yes."

Mother Wyse looked astounded, and made the sign of the cross. "I didn't know, Weasel. Why didn't Valvasor say he was sending me an angel?"

"But Sam wasn't an angel!" cried Denzil. "She was just an ordinary girl."

"Ordinary?" said Mother Wyse. "Agapantha was ordinary?"

"Well . . . not quite ordinary. But she wasn't an angel."

"Perhaps she gave Emmeline some wondrous medicine, such as they must make in her far-off world," suggested Mother Wyse.

"I didn't see her bring anything except her angel costume, her wings, and Murgatroyd," said Denzil, chewing his thumbnail. "Unless . . . oh, gawd, Jesus, Mary, forgive us! It *was* Him! It *was* the Christ Child we had, who made the marvel! Must have been! And I called Him a noisy little beggar, and said if He didn't shut up I'd put Him to sleep with Mother Gurtler's chickens! Oh, Battybird! He'll strike me dead with lightning! He'll make the earth open up and swallow me! He'll —"

Mother Wyse started to laugh. "Oh, Weasel," she cackled, rocking with mirth, her eyes streaming, "Weasel, didn't you know?"

"Know what?" asked Denzil, puzzled, thinking the old woman really had gone mad.

"Didn't they tell you, dearie? Oh, what a hoot!"

And she started chuckling again, throwing her

apron over her face, and wiping the tears from her eyes.

"*Know what?*" yelled Denzil.

Mother Wyse choked on a laugh, then tried to compose herself.

"I suppose you didn't have all that much to do with the Holy Child," she said.

"I gave him milk when he got hungry," said Denzil. "I suppose he won't strike me dead for that."

"You didn't have anything else to do with him?"

"No. Sam and Valvasor did all the rest."

"You didn't notice, then," said Mother Wyse, starting to laugh again. "Oh, Weasel. Your Christ Child was a *girl!*"

Denzil got such a shock he fell off his stool. Mother Wyse started chortling again. Offended, Denzil got up and went over to her kitchen corner. He stuck his fingers in a jar of honey, and licked them clean.

"I don't think it's funny," he said. For a while he was silent, thinking. Then he slowly turned around, and asked: "If my magic didn't do it, and Sam didn't do it, and the Christ Child was a girl, then who *did* do the miracle for Emmeline?"

Mother Wyse got up and stirred the stew in the cauldron. "Who knows?" she said. "There are greater marvels in the world than telephones, Connecting-Words, and magic spells. Human faith is a wonderful thing, Weasel. A wonderful thing." She dipped the spoon in the cauldron again, tasted it, and frowned.

"Not quite ready yet," she murmured. "While we're waiting, you could get that spare cauldron from the corner over there, take it outside, and fill it with snow. Then bring it back in, put it over the fire, and heat yourself some water."

"What for?" asked Denzil.

"It's Christmas," said Mother Wyse. "You know what happens at Christmas."

"Presents," he said. "We give each other presents. Valvasor and I got you a new pair of stockings. Purple, with pinky spots."

"Very nice, they'll be," said Mother Wyse. "I quite like kinky plots. But I wasn't talking about gifts, Weasel. I was talking about your Christmas treat. Your bath."

"Oh, no! I've had three of those this year! At Sam's. Honest. Cross-my-heart-and-hope-to-die! *Three!* I don't need —"

Mother Wyse picked up the spare cauldron, and put it firmly down in front of him.

"Bath time, Weasel," she said. "If you cause me any trouble, I'll make a lake outside, and throw you in it with a cake of soap and a scrubbing-brush. Now move!"

Grumbling, Denzil picked up the cauldron and went outside.

"This isn't natural," he muttered, as he scooped up snow with a small shovel, and loaded it into the cauldron. "I'll lose all my skin. My toenails will go soft, and fall off. My hair will break at the roots . . ."

Suddenly he stood up straight, his face intent and thoughtful. He went inside and said to Mother Wyse: "Mother Wyse? If you made that lake outside, with the soap and scrubbing-brush and all, do you think you could make the water warm?"

"Storm?" she said, and began chanting:

"These magic things I now do make:
A hole, a bath, a frozen lake,
A violent storm, with ice and sleet,
A brush to clean the boy child's feet,
An axe to help him break the ice,
And soap, to scrub away the lice.
And while the winds the wilds do freeze,
Let the boy child scrub his knees — "

Denzil gave a howl of dismay, shot outside again, and began frantically filling the cauldron. He was working so hard and so fast, he didn't hear Mother Wyse chuckling as she finished the spell:

"These magic things I now unmake,
And ask just this, for Weasel's sake:
That water's warm, near cosy hearth,
And let the boy enjoy his bath."

And, strangely, Denzil did.